Peter Heller

THE ORCHARD

Peter Heller is the national bestselling author of *Burn, The Last Ranger, The Guide, The River, Celine, The Painter*, and *The Dog Stars. The Painter* was a finalist for the *Los Angeles Times* Book Prize and won the prestigious Reading the West Book Award, and *The Dog Stars* has been published in twenty-six languages to date. Heller is also the author of four nonfiction books, including *Kook: What Surfing Taught Me About Love, Life, and Catching the Perfect Wave*, which was awarded the National Outdoor Book Award for Outdoor Literature. He holds an MFA from the Iowa Writers' Workshop in poetry and fiction, and he lives in Denver, Colorado.

ALSO BY PETER HELLER

FICTION

Burn

The Last Ranger

The Guide

The River

Celine

The Painter

The Dog Stars

NONFICTION

Kook: What Surfing Taught Me About Love, Life, and Catching the Perfect Wave

The Whale Warriors: The Battle at the Bottom of the World to Save the Planet's Largest Mammals

Hell or High Water: Surviving Tibet's Tsangpo River

Set Free in China: Sojourns on the Edge

THE ORCHARD

THE ORCHARD

Peter Heller

VINTAGE CONTEMPORARIES
Vintage Books
A Division of Penguin Random House LLC
New York

FIRST VINTAGE BOOKS EDITION 2025

Published by Vintage Books,
a division of Penguin Random House LLC,
1745 Broadway, New York, NY 10019.

Vintage is a registered trademark and Vintage Contemporaries and colophon are trademarks of Penguin Random House LLC.

The Cataloging-in-Publication Data is on file at the Library of Congress.

Vintage Contemporaries Trade Paperback ISBN: 979-8-217-00844-5
eBook ISBN: 979-8-217-00845-2

Book design by Soonyoung Kwon

penguinrandomhouse.com | vintagebooks.com

Printed in the United States of America
2nd Printing

The authorized representative in the EU for product safety and compliance is Penguin Random House Ireland, Morrison Chambers, 32 Nassau Street, Dublin DO2 YH68, Ireland, https://eu-contact.penguin.ie.

To Becky Arnold.
And to George and Laura Heller of Putney, Vermont.
From whose porch the world unfolded.

THE ORCHARD

Prologue

The file is in a small maple chest which has served as a lamp-stand for years, in the corner of my library. The chest is my mother's. Hayley. I remember that there are other keepsakes in the dove-jointed box: a deed to the cabin in Vermont; a hair ribbon and silk corsage from somebody's wedding, not hers; a tin of surf wax; a fountain pen; a simple green jade bracelet. A short scroll with the ink brush figure of a heron in bamboo and Chinese calligraphy in the corner.

That I could have forgotten the file, or ignored it, or delayed reading it for two decades. That I did not open the chest in all that time, that I was not willing.

Open the chest.

I lift off the lamp and carry the box to my desk and untape the key from the bottom and fit it into the wrought-iron keyhole. Why now? Because four days ago I found out that I was ten weeks pregnant—father known but at this point immaterial.

A daughter, I'm sure.

And somehow I feel that she would want to know who her grandmother was. And I feel, too, that in seeing what there is to see I might find my footing in a lineage that would ground me, that might whisper, "These are your people. Hard-boned and just, except to themselves. Who could never accept the wonder of their own magic."

But I also know that what I see could sear beyond hope of recovery.

*

The January blizzard shakes the panes in the French doors and drifts snow on the patio and against the low stone wall. Only midafternoon, but already going to a stormy dusk. I take a breath and turn the key and lift the top.

Not Pandora's box exactly, but an opening on a world I had preferred to keep closed. And there, beneath everything, under all the mementos like a false bottom, lies the manila file. I work it up one side of the box and let the other things slide gently back into place. I set it on the green blotter.

There is no title, no scrawl in Hayley's erratic hand, cursive so heedless and jumpy it's hard to believe that even she could read it. No writing, only the blank beige of the file folder in which I see the flat sands of a desert.

Do I wish that? That the file will contain nothing but the grains of lost time? Maybe. That I could handle. But beauty, as transmuted through the heart of my mother, may be too much to bear. And I know, I *know*, that inside this folder, from the first sheet to the last, there will be a devastating dose of the stuff. Because Hayley was, I found out years after it was too late to acknowledge in her company, one of the greatest English translators of the Tang dynasty, of the Chinese mountain poets and particularly of the princess Li Xue, who lived in western Sichuan in the beginning of the eighth century and was a contemporary of Li Po.

How can paper age so, inside a wooden box? The manila feels fragile in my fingers as I lift the edge and fold it back and see on top, on notebook paper with faded lines, the very first poem.

The Orchard

Tonight the scent of apple blossoms
and the murmur of the brook
slip through the open window
the way we once heard ten strings.
Our daughter sleeps despite the racket in my heart.

When you rode off, we were practically children.
I counted the months by the moon,
filled out like her, like a loom fan.
Every evening I stood at the gate.
The wind came from the west, but never brought news
of you.

Now our daughter is five and we are far from the capital.
I pray that the war has left you unscathed,
that you simply decided you no longer love me.
Death is permanent.
This way, one day you might have a change of heart,
and someone could tell you where to find us
in the blue hills above the river at Xinxiang.

Oh, God. Only the first. I slide the papers forward and breathe. I can see it, how she might order the work: Li Xue had left over five hundred poems and Hayley had selected thirty—will her translations be chosen for moments in time, to mirror in some way our own lives?

One

My mother was a back-to-the-lander. She had had this idea: to move with me, her six-year-old, to a cabin in a defunct orchard a few miles from a large river in Vermont. "Defunct" meaning that the trees had gone untended for years, had grown twisted and rangy, had yielded to waist-high orchard grass, young spruce and poplar, birch, maple. Or they had died and toppled, been lightning-struck and broken by the errant twisters that touched down, strangely, in these hills every few years.

The pond at the bottom of the orchard, brook-fed, had halfway silted in, but still held enough water to support the visits of giant beavers who seemed to me as big as bears and much meaner. In the stack of children's books Hayley brought with us there were *Winnie the Pooh* and *Corduroy*, and the bears were always nice.

The cabin was thirty-one and a half feet long and seventeen feet seven inches deep. I know because I now live in it half the time and I just took a tape to the outside walls. This seems to me to be an eccentric pairing of dimensions, but I suppose that the size of the logs dictated the length of the walls. In any event it was small, even for the two of us and Bear, our Bernese mountain mutt. This was Hayley's delusion of pedigree. To me he looked more like a combination of a beagle and a not-so-great Dane, with a lot of fur thrown in, errantly, for good measure. He was a happy mess, appearance-wise.

Hayley had been, at a very young age, an associate professor and a towering translator. Why did she give it all up to move here? Well, she gave part of it up: She never stopped working on her translations. I think in some way she was emulating the life of her subjects—the exile to the mountains, sometimes self-imposed, of the Tang dynasty poets. There was something they had all been seeking, and I think she was looking for it too.

Childhood memories are subject to constant revision, and so I have mostly vague and gauzy recollections of our move, punctuated by images and events that are far more crisp, even cinematic. I remember, for instance, the night the woodstove caught the roof on fire, and there is a certain pungency of resin-rich boards and scorched steel sheeting that still seems to linger in the recesses of my sinuses. At bonfires, when planks of construction scrap are thrown on, I find myself beginning to hyperventilate. Not exactly Proust's madeleine. Another vivid memory is the time I caught my first fish in the pond. This fish, which had to be a brook trout and could not have been more than six or seven inches long, looms in my mind like a plesiosaur. The fight to bring him in, which I conducted masterfully under the screaming instruction of my excited mother, lives in my memory with the grandeur of *The Old Man and the Sea*. Such is the wonder of youth, that the world is essentially malleable, that small events can be made big and large events made to disappear.

Hayley—Mom—was a woman of letters, an organic gardener, an artist, an ethical consumer, and thus prone to bouts, seasons, even eras, of delusion. This seems a harsh judgment, much harsher than is necessary, and probably wrong. What I mean is that she brought us, Bear and me, to this bucolic, decaying, ramshackle setting to make a new life close to nature; that nature was one leg of the stool, and self-sufficiency and beauty the others. This was a place where her little daughter and her dog would grow under the domain of the constellations, the fresh winds of the new seasons, and ripening apples and falling leaves and swelling brooks and thawing ice and phalanxes of migrating geese barking out of the high dark and and and . . .

Well, it was beautiful. It is. I can stand on my front porch and concur and thank her.

*

She thought she would revive the orchard. There were plenty of apples. They had been ripening and falling on their own for decades. The wildness had somehow concentrated their sweetness. I suppose it was because so many of the branches had died—prey to insects and disease—that the ones that were left and still bore fruit were in some way more distilled. Each ripe apple from these gnarled elders was a gift of deliciousness. I remember that. And I can still find a half-feral survivor, an impossibly twisted hybrid at the edge of what field remains, and bite through the ruddy skin with the same surprise and pleasure I did when I was seven.

The problem is that to make an orchard economically viable, one needs to produce a certain number of apples per tree, so that picking becomes efficient, and one needs pickers and pruners. But the pickers will shun you when they take one look at your sparse and ancient relics, as they know that they can harvest bumper crops just down the road.

And so, if you are a young, earnest back-to-the-lander with a tiny, as yet nonjudgmental daughter and a dog, you are relegated by your own impulsiveness to harvesting these trees on your own. And the bushels of spotted fruit which cost you so much scratched skin and backache and sunburn, and exhaust you entirely, and bring you nearly—sometimes not so nearly—to tears as you load them into the back of your balking mule of a pickup—these baskets fetch you, from the indulgent if tight-lipped buyer at the co-op, just enough money to pay for your gas and for new sneakers for your growing daughter. This buyer, by the way, was named Bill—Bill the Buyer, we called him—and he turned out to be a very sweet castaway whose family had all been killed in Croatia, and who informed us that our discolored, sometimes scabbed apples were "noncompliant" but "happily sweet."

So after that first fall, Hayley had to devise another plan. She was very good with a chainsaw and had cut enough dead apple trees to keep us in fragrant firewood for the next two winters. And as the blizzards raged and the icicles extended their glass fingers from the eaves and the forest behind the cabin creaked, the three of us gathered around the plank table in the middle of our one superheated room and put our heads together to figure out how we were going to make a living.

I must have turned seven, as my birthday is in January. I remember more than anything the grown-up feeling of putting fist under chin or against forehead while we pondered our future, while we brainstormed and strategized. I also remember the morning Hayley dressed me in my Monday Best, as she called it, and took me down to some big brick building in Brattleboro where a man with one eye that looked at the ceiling asked me a bunch of questions and gave Hayley a stack of notebooks, some heavy textbooks, and a calendar. He was the homeschooling superintendent, and he kept patting the corner of his mouth and one nostril with a handkerchief, and I later wrote a story called "Leaky Man" starring him. He shook Hayley's hand, patted me on the head, gave me a grape Tootsie Pop, and walked us to the door of his office, where he seemed very glad to get rid of us. Funny what you recall.

Two

This story begins in earnest the morning Rose Lattimore walked up the orchard track. It was mud season, mid-March, also sugaring time, when the nights freeze and the trees creak like old hinges, but then the days thaw, the brooks rush, the snow melts, and the sap runs in the maple trees. Like our neighbors, we tapped our maples. We endeavored to collect the faintly sweet-tasting water in hanging buckets, the old way. All our neighbors used plastic tubing which ran from tree to tree in awful webs.

Hayley kept the door and all the windows open and the woodstove roaring and boiled down the sap in a giant canning pot. Not quite the way our neighbors did it, with their dedicated sugarhouses and vast boiling pans, but it seemed to work. After what seemed to me years of strenuous gathering, we wrung about twenty gallons of ambrosia-like syrup out of the maples around the orchard. I wonder now if the reward for all of this wasn't supposed to be the work itself, but I am also cognizant of the fact that I had one pair of overalls and only two pairs of shoes: black-and-yellow fireman's boots with big looping hand-pulls and patches of glue that looked like spilled egg whites, and one pair of Keds that I despised because they were pink. And so one afternoon when Hayley was hammering together a crude chicken coop, I used a black magic marker to turn them into what I imagined were the paws of a tiger. I thought one could do anything on striped feet.

This one morning in late March, the woodstove was popping, the door was open, the nuthatches were wheezing. I was sitting below the porch steps on Bear, who often consented to be chair, backrest, pillow, ottoman, and, today, throne. I was Aud, Queen of the Vikings. I was seated before my ancestral lands and pulling on Bear's ear and asking him, as my chief warrior, Ragnar, where we should invade next, when I saw a flash of red down by the pond, at the bottom of the four-wheel-drive track that served as our long driveway.

I was only seven, but I could read like a wizard, and Hayley and I had been tearing through *The Curse of Andvari's Ring* together. Certain words like *eviscerate* I always needed help with, but I appreciated, after the halting effort, how the word tumbled out like so many guts. I usually didn't like being a girl so much—unlike me and Hayley, they seemed in stories to spend too much time inside castles, brushing their hair—but when we read about Gunnhild and Aud, I saw the possibilities in being a forthright and cruel queen.

Through the leafless trees, that first flash of red. A fleeting tatter of color lost again in the branches like the flight of a cardinal. Then it reappeared as a scarf—rose, not red—appended to a long purplish cardigan atop which bobbed a head of wild blond curls that spilled to broad shoulders and framed, I saw as she came closer, a red-cheeked face and hexagonal rimless glasses.

Bear and I fell silent. She saw us and waved and I waved back, twisting my hand like a queen. We didn't have a TV, but now I spent a day a week down at the elementary school in the village so that—as Hayley said, tying the waist bow on my only dress and patting me down—I didn't grow up like Tarzan. This was a poor rhetorical feint, as I couldn't think of anything better than growing up like Tarzan. Anyway, I had seen the marriage of Princess Diana and Prince Charles on the classroom TV and I knew how queens waved.

The lady responded with more enthusiasm. In fact, she stopped dead and waved with both arms, like a castaway to a passing ship. Bear and I glanced at each other. I could feel him stirring beneath me and hear his tail whisking the grass and I thumped his big head and commanded, "Stay!"

She came on. When she got abreast of our old truck she stopped and said, "Does he bite?"

"Definitely," I said.

"He doesn't look mean."

"He's not mean, he just bites."

"I see."

The lady was of indeterminate age. She seemed both much older and much younger than Hayley. Her eyes were a mischievous glancing blue.

"Well," she said. "Requesting permission to speak to the queen."

My hand reached up and felt the gold cardboard crown we had made yesterday in first grade. It was a stupid crown, nothing like a Viking queen's, but still. Bear couldn't restrain himself any longer and stood up and upended me. I scrambled to my feet.

"Are you from Brattleboro?" I said. Brattleboro was the seat of all officialdom.

"Westminster West," she said.

"Oh."

Bear was prancing in place and whining with excitement and trying not to jump on the lady. I thumped him on the head and said, "Bear, *sit!*" He sat. She stuck out her hand, which was too much for him. He squirmed and covered her fingers with slobber.

"Rosie," she said.

"Oh," I said. "Bear, quit!"

"What's your name?"

"Frith."

"Frith!" Her voice rang like the brass bell that hung on the porch and that Hayley struck to call me to dinner. She had very white, even teeth. I wondered if she was in the movies. Nobody had ever said my name with such delight. It kind of floated up between us, then flew away into the trees. "Like in *The Snow Goose*," she said.

"Yep."

I was charmed, I admit it. "You want to speak to Hayley?" I said.

"Okay."

"Moooooommmmm!" I screamed.

*

Rosie was a weaver who actually made a decent living at her craft. Or art. Once when we were fishing with chicken gizzards and bobbers (lame), she told me that the only difference between art and craft, or art and conversation, or art and humming—or even fishing—is the maker's connection to God. I had no idea what she was talking about, but that line has stuck with me all my life. I am not a religious person, but I think she was onto something. Rosie often said odd things at odd times, which now seem freighted with some kind of genius, or foresight.

On that bright morning, with visible steam pouring out of the windows, she put one slender hand against the doorframe and yelled "Knock, knock!" and thus began what I think of as the third chapter of our lives, the first two being my arrival on the planet and Hayley and me moving to the orchard.

*

Rosie had heard of us through her friend Ivy Darrow, who ran the next orchard down the hill, toward the river. A real orchard, with farm trucks painted with a logo of apple-cheeked maidens spilling red and green apples from bushel baskets while the Vermont hills turned purple behind them. The bushel baskets that caused Hayley so much distress to fill. Hayley, I thought, whenever I saw those trucks rumble by, didn't look a thing like those maidens, and I wondered if it was a character flaw. The hills did look like our own distant hills going blue in the evening, and I appreciated that some of the apples in the picture were green, like our own apples, and this verisimilitude strengthened my conviction that there was something seriously awry with our operation.

Rosie had gone to school with Ivy since they were around seven, my age. And one evening, drinking gin and tonics on Ivy's porch, Ivy said, "I have new neighbors. In Gray's old cabin."

"Hippies, I bet," Rosie said, which was a bit unfair, a bit calling the kettle black.

"Sort of. She was a professor, apparently. In something like translation. Has a book, sort of a classic."

"She?"

"It's just the woman, Hayley, and her daughter. Who is little. Super nice. They don't have a phone, of course, so I told them they're welcome to give my number out to family and use mine for emergencies."

Rosie said later that the notion of an author of any stripe living right next door was just too tempting. She was wrestling at the time with her own identity as an artist, so a translator of Chinese poetry, and therefore herself a poet of sorts, was maybe an irresistible draw.

What she saw when she half entered the cabin cannot have been inspiring. Hayley's head was in the scalding steam over the five-gallon pot as she tried to fish a hydrometer out of what she hoped was nearly bona fide syrup. The hydrometer measured density, and it was like a little buoy thermometer you floated in the hot sap. When the red line on the tube rose even with the surface of the liquid, you had syrup. That's when she usually yelled, "Eureka!" Hayley's head was wrapped in a rag to keep her hair out of the pan, and she was shirtless—why get a shirt soaked with steam? Her bra policy was inconsistent, and she would never deign to own a bikini when one clearly was meant to swim in one's birthday suit, so today her breasts were bare. She wore a long skirt patched with what looked like tear sheets from a Marvel comic but were actually patches cut from a child's Superwoman bed ruffle that Tina at the thrift store had given her for free the last time we were there. Hayley did not look like an associate professor. She looked like a witch at her kettle.

How she kept her face from burning in the steam, I don't know. "*Fuck!*" she yelped as she dropped the hydrometer back in the pot, and then she picked up a rag and lifted the heavy vessel off the range and set it on the plank floor.

This was pretty much how all our living-off-the-land endeavors played out.

Mom blew a strand of stray hair out of her face and then sneezed—turning away from the bucket of precious nectar at her feet—and when she sneezed I saw with acute embarrassment that her boobs bounced. In moments of vulnerability, I thought of her as Mom. But those moments always scared me, and so I liked her much better as Hayley. When she turned back, she realized that she had a visitor. She grabbed a torn towel off the back of a wooden chair and covered herself and, holding the towel together in front with one hand, said, "Excuse me, Jesus."

"Gesundheit," Rosie said.

"Thanks."

There was an awkward face-off, and then Hayley said, "Who the fuck are you?"

*

Rosie, to her credit, laughed. An honest laugh that seemed to clear the steam from the room and make Hayley look less like a witch.

"I the fuck am Rosie." She stuck out her hand, which Hayley uncertainly took.

"Are you from child welfare?"

"God, no. Nor the IRS. Nor Alcohol, Tobacco, and Firearms. I don't think I would have gotten past the child or the dog."

"Harmless. The dog, I mean."

"He doesn't bite?"

"He barely chews his food." Hayley saw me behind the woman's skirts. "She, the little whippet behind you—well, the jury's out. Just a sec." Hayley turned and snatched a T-shirt off the same chair and slipped it over her head. "Let's sit outside," she said. "The bench is in the sun."

It was one of those early spring days that are cold in the shade and warm in the sun. Sun in Vermont is not the same threat it is in, say, Colorado, or Chihuahua, and is usually welcome. The bench was scooched to the front edge of the little porch, where it could catch every ray. We all sat on it, Rosie in the middle. That's when I realized how tall our visitor was, and how strong. When you have been sitting next to one woman your whole life, you get used to the topography. It's like living all your days at the skirt of a certain mountain. So when you are suddenly beside another mountain that is much taller and more formidable, well. It startled me. I looked up at Rosie and noticed the breadth of her shoulders, the strength in her hands. I leaned out and looked at Mom, the top of whose head came to about Rosie's jawline. Hayley was no slouch. Once she wiped the tears from her eyes, she could grit her teeth and heft a bushel of apples as well as any woman.

But I knew immediately, sitting next to Rosie and feeling the sun's heat radiate off her mohair sweater and smelling the fragrance of another adult woman, that this apparition would not grit her teeth when she swung a bushel basket. She would whistle without breaking a note.

"Hmm," Rosie said, though about what I wasn't sure. "I remember this orchard when the Darrows still ran it."

"We still pick," Hayley said. "A few of the trees."

"The apples are noncompliant," I said.

Rosie laughed. "The best things often are," she said.

"You want a beer?" Mom said.

"Sure."

Hayley got up and brought out two cans of Catamount and one of A&W root beer. I heard three sharp sighs as the three tabs were pulled back, and then we all drank in silence in the sun. If anyone thought it odd that Rosie seemed to be here for no stated reason, no one said anything. Sitting in a row on the bench, drinking our beers, seemed suddenly to be as good as it gets. I swung my legs and for once didn't feel the need to cause havoc or be somewhere else in my imagination. Finally Rosie said, "Ivy tells me you're a translator. Or so trained."

Or so trained. Lovely.

Mom choked. She put her fist up and coughed into it. "Wrong way," she gasped. She pounded her breastbone. "Translator, whew."

"No?" Rosie said.

"I have translated. Seems like another life." Which wasn't exactly true. I saw Hayley at night when I was supposed to be asleep, sitting at the table with the lantern and writing in her notebook.

Rosie waited. "The poetry of the Tang," Hayley said. "Even published a volume. But."

"But," Rosie repeated.

We all blinked into the sunlight and tipped back our cans and looked out into the leafless orchard where the last patches of snow were melting into the runnels of the tire tracks, the shoots of green grass, the mud. The two *buts* seemed to encompass and embrace the old apple trees, the hills beyond, the garble of the brook, the dropping two-note song of a chickadee. It was not like a bad thing; I remember feeling that nothing was bad at the moment. The *buts*, I mean. Hayley's quiet acknowledgment of surrender—to this life, to raising me. The barely regretful relinquishment of much of her literary past.

"And you?" Hayley said.

"I have woven. Blankets and stuff. Shawls. And work hard at soft sculptures that, frankly, may be awful."

The three of us laughed. I don't think I had any idea why I was laughing. I had never seen a soft sculpture, unless you counted my plush lobster. Who gives their kid a plush lobster? I think it explains a lot.

"I'm sure they're spiff," Hayley said. "Did you knit your cardigan?"

"Yes. Well . . ."

Hayley raised an eyebrow and raised her can in a toast. We all clinked. I don't think people pay enough attention to the momentous times in our lives when nothing happens. Nobody spoke. I leaned into the new woman because the sun on the soft mohair was irresistible. Softness and heat and a smell like maybe the Andes and maybe wild roses, though I wouldn't have known what either of those smelled like. Before this we lived in Denver with Pop. Pop had a Cajun food truck and was, according to Hayley, a heroin addict. When I was really little, the plush lobster was the closest thing they could find to a crawdad.

So, Nothing Happening: discuss. As I might now challenge my literature students at Amherst on a pop quiz. *Quiz* is the wrong word. I often hit them with little essay prompts at the beginning of class just to check in on the patient, so to speak. How *is* the fragile faculty of critical thinking faring today? Often not so well. Sometimes I tell them to please not put a name at the top and to cut loose. *Professor Cormier, with all due respect, how the f@#k can I discuss nothing when there is Nothing to discuss? Not being clever. Sincerely, Mystified in Massachusetts.* I love these. I'll collect them and read a bunch aloud to raucous laughter. Hayley, who always thought school was for zombies, would approve.

It was nice to have company. Bear liked it. He lay curled at our feet on the sun-warmed planks, half over Rosie's lightweight hiking boots. A horsefly buzzed, I could smell the muddy sweetness of wet earth sponging up the thaw, and I could hear water trickling away from a hundred runnels in the ground. I tipped back my root beer and let the exquisite syrup sift through my teeth and effervesce against the roof of my mouth. I usually got a can of root beer only on Sundays.

In the nothing that was happening, I was experiencing a certain whirring recalibration, which sounds, I imagine, like the muted shuffling of a deck of cards. I was adjusting to the company of another, apparently strong, woman, and to the alchemy of laughter.

Because I realized, for maybe the first time, that Hayley rarely laughed. In those minutes of nothing happening, my system was acclimatizing to an atmosphere with less gravity, in which the usual hopping thoughts might transmute into bounding flight. Sitting on the bench in the sun with these two women, I had a taste for the first time of what it might feel like to believe anything was possible.

What I may have understood was that life with Hayley was kind of heavy. It felt like a fight for survival every day, because

I guess that's what it really was. Even the lighter moments—making blueberry pie and getting it smeared all over our faces, catching a brook trout who didn't want to be caught as badly as I wanted to catch it, jumping off Jumping Rock into the pond, playing cribbage by the light of the Aladdin lantern—all those moments took place in that context of survival. They were relief. Respite. Could a seven-year-old be aware of all that? She could certainly feel it.

I leaned into the woman and sucked the root beer down to the last drop.

"If you all want to see my sculptures in person, why don't you come by?" Rosie said.

I sat up. "When?" I said.

"Tomorrow. I only live fifteen minutes away."

"We have a slow truck," Hayley said.

"Oliver," I piped. "Named for the tortoise."

"Ha!" Rosie laughed. "That's like the old Vermont joke where the Texan brags about his ranch!"

We both looked at her.

"Haven't heard it?" We both shook our heads. Jokes weren't really our forte. "The Texas rancher is bragging to his Vermont buddy about how big his ranch is. He says, 'I can drive four hours and still not get to the edge of my property!' The

Vermonter says, 'I had a car like that once too. Sold it.'" We didn't laugh. We grinned, though.

"Not funny?" Rosie said.

"It's the best," I said, and swung my legs for punctuation. "Tell us another one."

"You sure?"

I leaned forward and looked at Hayley. She had an expression I don't think I had ever seen. She was looking out into the bare trees of the orchard but not really looking at anything, just smiling in this almost bewildered way, like she was soaking up the extreme pleasantness of waiting for a joke. Or feeling the March sun on her face with no chore to do at the moment. Free from worry, for just a minute. I knew in every cell that our lives, mine and Hayley's, were boundlessly rich, and better in their purity and self-sufficiency than most everyone else's, and yet I was suddenly aware of how lean they were. I almost yelled, "Tell it!"

"Okay, okay. It's R-rated. I don't think you'll get it." I had no idea what she was talking about.

"*Please,*" I pleaded.

"Okay," she said. "So this old lady got on the Amtrak train at White River Junction and sat next to an old farmer. It was the Boston Express. She said, 'What are you going to Boston for?' He said, 'My granddaughter is graduating from Tufts.' 'Oh, that's nice,' she said." Rosie made old lady and old man voices with thick Vermont accents.

" 'What are you going down for?' the farmer asked.

" 'Oh, I go down every Friday to the fish market to get scrod.' The farmer stared at her for a second.

" 'Why, lady,' he said finally, 'I've heard it every which way, but I ain't never heard it in the past pluperfect!' "

Hayley burst into laughter. She actually dropped her almost empty can onto the porch, where it rolled off the edge. I had never heard such an utterance come from her lungs. Free, unadulterated, joyous laughter. I let my can drop too and kicked it a little so it rolled off the porch, and I made sounds of extreme hilarity. I had no clue what the joke was about, but I loved the way she did the old people.

"Good, right?" Rosie said.

"Oh, man, good," I said when I had caught my fake lost breath. Which made Hayley lean forward and survey me, and that set her off on even more raucousness. I wasn't sure if I should be pleased or proud, so I pounded on Bear's head and yelled, "Bear, *sit!*" He'd gotten up in all the excitement and was knocking everyone's knees.

"Whew!" Hayley said. "I don't know if the joke is the funniest thing I've ever heard or if, sadly, even the suggestion of getting laid once a week seems profligate!" (Admittedly, I could never have remembered these words, having zero context. Thankfully, years later, Rosie helped me reconstruct the conversation.)

"Hear, hear," Rosie said and raised her beer can, which was the only one that hadn't rolled to the ground.

*

We did go to Rosie's studio the next day. We had no electricity—we used kerosene lamps at night and had a small propane fridge—but there was running water, gravity-fed from the spring up the hill, and a little gas-powered on-demand hot-water heater on the wall and two standing propane tanks in back of the cabin. So that morning we both took hot baths, which we allowed ourselves twice a week. At other times, if the pond was free of ice, we'd jump in, however cold it was outside. Hayley said I was part seal. I can still swim in coastal Maine, and frolic around like it's the Caribbean, which amazes whoever I'm with.

It's funny how simply, how quickly the lens can change through which we view our day, our lives. Fleets of dark clouds with bruised bellies flew across the sun, and yet that morning seemed brighter and somehow more vivid than the ones before. The brook burbled more gaily. The vireos and kiskadees and flycatchers, all just coming into the country again after their sojourns to the south, sounded more exuberant. Hayley hummed as she filled the tub.

We still, neither of us, knew what we were doing. We didn't have a clue as to why Rosie had shown up in the first place, why she had sat with us and told us stories, why she'd invited us over. Maybe she just liked us. Despite our struggles, I think we felt likable. Lovable even. But she'd come over before she knew that. Why? She was a friend of Ivy's, our neighbor. Maybe she was just curious.

As a seven-year-old, I'm sure I was more able to simply accept these mysteries than Hayley, but one of the things I love about my mother in retrospect is that she had that child-like capacity as well. She could be accepting of the gifts that came her way without the second-guessing that so many of us endure. If I brought her a haphazard bouquet of asters and pea flowers and Indian paintbrush, with all the reds bunched to one side and a white umbrella of Queen Anne's lace sticking awkwardly out the top, her hazel eyes would darken with emotion and her cry of "How totally, utterly gorgeous!" would ring with zero irony, and her hug would be strong and full of more gratitude than I might experience now, as an adult, in a month of keeping score. It's a rare talent. Maybe her genius. So yes, life was hard, often scary—as when we discovered a large leak in the roof in a February thaw and had no money to fix it. But I had nothing to compare it to and so swam in our daily challenges as a fish swims through water. As far as I was concerned, roofs leaked in the middle of a hard winter, clothes were washed by hand in a steel tub, and mothers spilled over with happiness when you handed them a fistful of flowering weeds. And so Rosie showed up, I guess, like a rangy bouquet, full of mixed scents and stems that were too long, and Hayley was happy to receive her.

She filled the tub with scalding water and nudged the cold-water valve that spouted very cold. She stirred with a plastic ladle and said, "You first." The ladle made me think of witches again. She had cracked the door on the woodstove to feed the fire more air, and it rushed and popped and warmed the room to July. That's how we measured the temperature. Hayley would say, "What do you think we should have tonight—September?" And I'd say, "November!" And she'd say, "We'll freeze, won't we? I don't think the quilts are thick enough. How about mid-October?" I'd nod and she'd tap-close the vent at the back of the stove a little more.

So now it was July warm and we were both in our birthday suits and I said, "Are you going to cook me like soup?"

"Weeelll . . ."

"You first!" I yelled. "To make sure!"

So she climbed in, one leg at a time, uttering, "Oh, oh, ooo . . ." and then I hopped in after her and we shared the tub. I loved that. It was crowded but more fun than bathing alone, which seemed like work. There was a plastic Dannon yogurt container, and I liked to fill it and dump it on her head and watch the water stream in her auburn hair.

We bathed and air-dried by the stove, and when we got hot we stood on the porch, steaming, and let the goosebumps gradually work up our arms. Our version of a sauna. Hayley dressed me in my Monday Best, the dress with the honeysuckle print, little flowers of orange and white on a yellow field, and she put on clean blue jeans and a white Mexican blouse with an embroidered neckline and she opened the tailgate for Bear, who hopped up without being told, and off we went, rattling down the driveway.

We were a team, indivisible, the nurturing going in all directions. A team of three.

*

There were two ways to get to the river, one down West Hill, past the Wattses' horses, the Cooper-Ellises' field, the Darrows' orchard, and the Grays' farm and through the village, and one down Tavern Hill, past the Carows' pastures, and then nothing but woods until the Westminster West Road. That's the one we took. It sounds like a children's book, doesn't it? The country that time forgot. Except that the North Country Raiders, an outlaw motorcycle group in constant war with the Hells Angels and the Diablos, had a clubhouse just up from the intersection of the county highway. There was an old barn into which went the motorcycles, a vinyl-sided, galleried, two-story house that looked like a spliced section of motel, and a horseshoe pit usually attended, winter and summer, by a half dozen giant bearded men holding red plastic cups. They always waved when we passed, and we always waved back. Hayley said they tried to be good local citizens and always gave money to the VFW pancake breakfast and the elementary school clothes drive, and even took a bullied autistic child to school on the back of a bike one day. "It keeps the local cops out of their face," she said.

"Why don't they take me to school?"

"You don't go to school."

"On Wednesdays." Suddenly, school sounded way more desirable.

She said, "Bear and I aren't good enough? And Oliver? You want a big bearded dude on a Harley?"

Today there were only four dudes playing horseshoes—it was still early—and they held coffee mugs, not beer, but they still waved.

"Why don't we get horseshoes?" I said.

Hayley double-clutched and downshifted at the stop sign, then lurched us back in the bench seat as she accelerated onto the Westminster West Road, which we did with a coughing roar the Raiders probably appreciated.

"Good idea," she said.

"They could come over and teach us."

"Well."

"Are they mean?"

"Not to us."

Now I know that the Raiders were a major conduit for heroin in our region of southern Vermont and had killed two dealers working for the Angels with croquet mallets, bikers-with-hearts-of-gold aside. There seemed to be many uses for yard games.

We drove. There were some big hayfields in the river bottom, stubbled with the first green shoots of timothy. We passed a roadside barn with a sign over the broad doors that said PUTNEY PLAYERS. I read it out loud. "What do they play?" I said.

"Plays," she said. "They're an acting troupe." I looked at her.

"A theater." I looked at her.

"Whoa," she said.

It dawned on her that I had never been to any kind of a play. I was pretty new to first grade, and only on Wednesdays at that. I hadn't yet been to a school Christmas pageant, or put on a play in class, or been to a school production of *Grease* (thank God) or *The Crucible*. I was uninoculated. A tabula rasa. I was the Ishi of West Hill, a true innocent, the last of my kind. I see myself standing on a rock above a brook in my Monday Best, all tattered, hair wild, holding a short bow, and murmuring a language that will be lost to the world when I pass. Not that I regretted being homeschooled, ever. I find that I can recognize other homeschooled souls in a crowd, almost as if there was a secret handshake or a tell; we have a certain temper of spirit that has been cooked out of everyone else.

Nor was my life free of drama for a second. I enacted my own theatrical productions, for which I enlisted Bear and Hayley and which could go on for days and days like one of those awful weeklong Shakespeare-in-the-round experiments for which there always seems to be grant money and an endless supply of actors willing to snatch sleep on cots like transoceanic airline pilots. I just didn't know what my creations were called.

Hayley swallowed hard and drove in silence for a while and kept glancing at me. I think maybe it was dawning on her how sheltered I was, even deprived. How far she had taken me in the pursuit of her bucolic idyll.

These moments of self-awareness can be a hammer blow to the psyche. *Am I the worst mom on earth?* she might have been thinking. *Am I a selfish monster? How on earth can I change course now?*

She might not have been thinking any of that. She might have been delighting in my immaculate ignorance, and in fresh plans to get me to Brattleboro to see *You Can't Take It with You*. Or *Steel Magnolias*. But wondering how we could afford tickets when the next propane refill was going to be touch-and-go.

She was not a horrible mom. She was doing her best. I was well fed; if I had one dress, well, it had honeysuckle flowers on it; we took a stack of books out of the village library every week and she read them all with me; and she bought a four-dollar six-pack of Catamount beer every week and rationed herself to one a day, minus Tuesdays. Not a monster.

Would I have rather chosen to live in a faux stone house on a cul-de-sac in a suburb of Lowell, Massachusetts, with a bus stop and a pack of other latchkey kids living on the street? And *SpongeBob* on Nickelodeon?

Well . . .

*

Westminster West, like Putney, has pretty much one main drag, with half a dozen short side streets and not a straight stretch of road anywhere, as the river and the tributary brooks and the hills wreak havoc with line of sight. There's a white clapboard church and a general store, but no town square. I go through the hamlet now quite often and it always has the feel that a flood came through carrying the smaller, more buoyant flotsam of rural New England and set it down along the drainages as the water receded. Everything in my memory of the place is slightly tilted, like a Dr. Seuss village, and I seriously wonder if there is a plumb wall anywhere.

Rosie did not live in town. Hayley handed me the torn-out notebook page with directions and asked me to read it. I did, slowly. "Turn left at Wilson Farm Road." We turned off the pavement and began to climb away from the river on a washboard dirt road. "Turn right at Charlie's Fo—"

"Forge."

"Forge." She did. We followed a stone wall and an open field that fell away below us with views across the river.

"What's a forge?"

"It's a very hot fire where a blacksmith works. What's a blacksmith?" I nodded. "He heats up metal in the coals and pounds it with a hammer and bends it into different shapes. Like horseshoes."

"Like what those mean men play? The ones who are nice to us?"

"Right."

Up ahead, the narrow road bent hard to the left, but an even narrower drive continued straight through two lines of stately old maples, at the end of which sat the prettiest house I'd ever seen.

It was bright yellow clapboard with blue window boxes and a greenhouse in the field below in which plants grew to the roof like some wild bit of jungle. Around the house were narrow terraces of river stone, and next to it towered a tall white pine. When Hayley cut the engine and we climbed out, I heard a stream and the wind rushing in the pine needles like the saddest whispery song. I was enchanted. It was everything our cabin wasn't. It was cultivated and neat and colorful. It felt prosperous. I noticed that behind the yellow house was another: not quite a playhouse but much smaller than the main, and of the same color and proportions, with the same white porch and blue door. That was it. I was gone.

We walked up mossy granite steps to the main door and Hayley knocked. One can tell a lot from the sound of a front door. I could hear the rap of Hayley's knuckles resonating in what must have been a large space, a space of hardwood and stone counters, and lots of air, where the knocks could echo freely and resound.

No answer, just the soughing of the pine. Hayley knocked again, this time the tattoo they call "Shave and a Haircut." Again the sound of echoey luxurious living spaces, not ours, and wind. And then a faint two-knock answer and the latch ticked and balked as if too stiff for the opener, and then the door swung inward, and a sudden recalibration as the Rosie I expected transmogrified into a small, very old woman with the softest, cleanest white hair. She was white from head to toe except for bright red lipstick and two rounds of rouge on her cheeks and the same glancing blue eyes as Rose. "Well, hello," she said softly. "So good to see you all. Rose has said *so* much about you. Come in, come in."

She had a strong southern accent, which was new to me. We hadn't heard her footsteps because she was wearing white tennis shoes that barely whispered on the hardwood floor and rugs. I took in the vast expanse of polished heartwood and the islands of rug scattered across it, the fantastic patterns in reds, golds, blues. There were birds and fish and twining vines and flowers I'd never seen. They led across the big open room to what evidently was a kitchen and a bank of big windows looking across the misty valley, and French doors leading out to the gardens. In the farthest corner of the room was a gleaming black grand piano.

We came in. If we hadn't really known what we were doing there before, we were even more disoriented now. She must have noticed our confusion. "I'm Marie," she said and lifted her hand. "Marie Bettencourt." Her hand was white like the rest of her, and when I took it, it was marvelously soft and dry, kind of dusty and fragrant. If a woman could be made out of baby powder, this was her. "I'm Rosie's aunt. Great-aunt, actually." She was ninety-three.

"And you are Frith, I believe, the Nordic Queen." She did not so much shake my hand as let me caress hers, which was cool and pulsing like the baby flicker we had found the summer before. She smiled. Her smile was soft and kind of powdery too, like it might blow away if we didn't shut the door. "And you are Hayley, the famous traductrix. So pleased."

With her small hand, she made the smallest gesture toward the kitchen end of the room, as if she was sweeping away a single strand of spider silk. She turned and led us across. It was only then that I noticed that she walked with a cane.

*

We went slowly, in a line, like the Three Magi. Hayley had read me the poem by Eliot. She was always reading me poems that were way over my head. In dispensing so much incomprehensible music, she taught me that I could fiercely love something I didn't understand in the least. Good practice for when you got to the really big things, like God.

So the three of us bent into an imaginary headwind and trekked across the vast sands of that wood floor, and I looked back over my shoulder and pretended I was leading a string of camels. When we got to the butcher block island she motioned to us again, this time to sit at the high stools. Marie leaned on her cane and kind of pivoted around it, and smiled her sweet powdery smile and said, "Would you like some Co-Cola? Or sweet tea? You must be terribly thirsty."

That seemed odd. Walking across the floor wasn't that tough, camels or no. Neither was the fifteen-minute drive from Putney. We weren't exactly dying of thirst. But I wasn't going to let Hayley do anything dumb like politely decline, so I blurted, "Is that like Coke?"

"It is Coke, dear."

"On the rocks!" I said and glanced quickly at Hayley, who was looking at me in horror.

"A:," Hayley said, "Say please. And B: Where on earth did you learn 'on the rocks'?"

"Watching TV at school on Wednesday. When you were an hour late to pick me up, remember?"

Hayley turned red. Marie blinked and smiled mildly and turned toward the gleaming stainless fridge.

*

After she'd served us Coke and iced tea, Marie sat on a stool across the island and hooked the handle of her cane over the edge of the butcher block. She said, "I prefer the stool to the easy chair, on account of . . . sometimes I just can't climb out of a chair. The other day I thought I'd have to call the fire department. Or mountain rescue. Wouldn't that be embarrassing? I think I'd die."

Hayley, who hadn't said one word except to scold me, sipped her tea and took in the room. I followed her eyes to a floor-to-ceiling bookshelf behind the piano and saw in her look an almost wolfish hunger. We couldn't read the spines from here, but I could see that many of the books were very tall, and I wondered if they were children's books.

Hayley said, "Marie, you're clearly not from here, or even New Hampshire. You have the loveliest accent."

Marie laughed. "New Hampshire! God, no. I still can't understand people from New Hampshire, can you? I mean the speech."

"Barely."

"I know. It's taken me forty years to grok Vermonters." She had a slight tremor; I noticed that her head shook minutely side to side. And that her face was oval and neat—not at all the broad, open face of her niece—and that she had pronounced cheekbones. She was kind of a stunner. "Now," she said, turning to me. "Frith. What do you enjoy most in all the world?"

Nobody had ever asked me that before. I had no stock lines, the way the Miss America contestants answered almost everything as if they were reading off of cue cards. A pageant rerun was one of the shows I'd watched after school the other day while Hayley was changing a flat tire. The girl I liked was from Montana.

"Fashion design and animal husbandry," I said.

Marie emitted a peal of laughter like a teakettle. Her light frame shook and shook until I was sure she'd collapse into a pile of scented talc. When she could find her voice she said, "I can certainly see why Rose adores you both, yes I can."

Hayley cleared her throat and said, "Marie, will Rosie be joining us?" I remember that. Somehow it stuck in my mind as very tactful and very unlike the way my mother usually spoke. Funny to see someone we think we know top to bottom change in another's company.

"Oh!" cried Marie, as if she'd left milk boiling in the pan. "I'd completely forgotten! You'd come to see Rose. And here I was, hogging you both to myself." She patted her forehead with a handkerchief that appeared from the sleeve of her cream sweater, a gesture not even in the same universe as those of Leaky Man. "She had to run to the vet. Kits, that's her little cat, had some sort of episode. She felt awful and said she didn't have your number, and she had no idea how long she'd be in Brattleboro, and she's absolutely mortified."

Did Hayley's face fall?—just the way my heart felt? If it did, she banished the frown with a bright smile. "Oh, I'm so sorry," Hayley said, again sounding different from my mother. "We hope it's not serious."

"Well, I don't know," Marie sighed with an abstraction that seemed philosophical. "Would you all like some lunch? Rose made lamb stew."

"Oh, thank you, no," Hayley said. "We'll be getting back. We have sap buckets overflowing." And with that, and a few more minutes of banter, Hayley gently extracted us from the congenial, if papery, hospitality of Marie Bettencourt.

*

At the truck, where Bear was being a good dog for once and sitting patiently in front of the grill, I looked longingly back at the neat yellow house with the blue door, and the grand piano and wall-to-ceiling bookshelves inside that looked to hold children's books. (They didn't; I found out later they were art books, from Aho and Banksy and Bonnard to Caravaggio to the Zen masters of the Edo period. They would later have a profound effect on my education.)

"How come we didn't stay for lunch?" I said.

"Cuz," Hayley said. "Get in."

I couldn't move. I was rooted, staring back at the house. "Cuz why?" I said.

"Cuz never take anything that's not offered freely."

"She offered it." I was zeroing in on the blue door as if it might be the gateway to some fairy kingdom. As far as I was concerned, it was. Then I surveyed the wide lawn, the terracing, the greenhouse, the view across the valley.

“Yeah but,” Hayley said.

“But what?”

“It wasn’t quite free. She kinda had to, didn’t she? Knowing we came all this way.”

“It wasn’t very far. Fifteen minutes.”

“Still. C’mon, let’s go. We’ll come back sometime, maybe.”

The “maybe” stung like a cut. I had just been totally enchanted; I had the sense that Hayley had been too. Could it be swept away that quickly? I felt like crying but girded myself. Hayley and I were a team; the way she said, “C’mon, let’s go,” reinforced it. We were in this together, we would face the disappointments of the world back to back.

I moved my lips around and kicked at the front tire. “Okay,” I said. “C’mon, Bear, let’s blow.” And we all got back in Oliver and rattled down the hill.

Three

I have found, in the wisdom of years, that the best relationships usually begin rocky. Rockily. Is that a word? It should be, given how much of life rolls that way. The man who ended up being my college boyfriend sank our canoe on our first date. He didn't really sink it, a moose did, a gigantic monster bull in rut who swam out a quarter mile to wage the attack. It was October, the water was very cold, the bull flailed his front hooves, and frankly I'm amazed no one died.

Having Rosie not be home was nowhere near as life-threatening, but in the hierarchy of memory, it seems more tragic.

"Shit happens," Hayley consoled as we drove past the cutoff back up Tavern Hill. "Let's go on into town and get a milkshake." She meant continue straight on into Putney, where our general store had a dairy counter in back. This was a treat beyond reckoning. I knew, even at seven, that we couldn't afford it. The collateral costs of heartbreak. We sat at the long, polished wooden bar and had chocolate malts. I can still taste it. The gritty, almost salty bits of toasted barley dissolving in my mouth with the blended ice cream. Hayley's tan and tendoned forearm touching mine. The bubbly suck of the straw as I ran it around the top edge of the shake.

"You know, Pup," Hayley said. "The people we are most excited about often hurt us, and they don't mean to. At all."

"How come?" I said, and blew out through the straw to make more bubbles.

"Because we are so crazy excited. And everyone, *everyone*, is just kinda poking along, doing the best they can."

"Oh," I said.

She leaned her head against mine and blew bubbles, too, into her glass.

"Right?" she said.

"Right," I said. Not sure exactly about what but feeling just then that it was good to have backup like Hayley.

"I translated a poem once by the very great and wonderful Chinese poet Li Po. Wanna hear it? It's really short."

I nodded, rubbing my head up and down against hers.

"Okay, it's about visiting his friend the monk up at the monastery on the mountain and he's not home. Like Rosie. It goes,

A dog's bark and the sound of water,
peach blossoms thicken in spring rain.
Deep in the pines, the deer move like shadows,
and at the creek I hear no temple bell.
The mist moves through wild bamboo.

A flying stream plummets from the jasper mountain.
No one knows where you have gone.
Sadly, I lean against a pine and write you this note."

"We heard a stream," I said. "But Bear didn't bark."

"Nope. Let's go home."

" 'K."

"Feel better?"

I nodded.

When we climbed our rocky track to the cabin and Oliver rolled to his customary stop against the half-buried rounded boulder and Bear hopped out and I saw a thread of pale smoke coming out of our stovepipe and the way the cloud shadows swept the orchard, I felt happy again and glad to be home. Almost as if we had been on a long trip. And the bright yellow house receded into the fairy world where I guessed it was meant to be.

Four

Rosie came back that afternoon, straight from the vet. She again parked her old Subaru down below, again walked up the track through the orchard. Today she was wearing a heather blue short zip jacket that had the density of felt. It was the most beautiful piece of clothing I'd ever seen. Also, it matched her eyes. She waved and waved as she came up. I wasn't sitting on Bear but trying to throw a horseshoe at a heavy stick we'd sharpened and hammered into the ground. It wasn't a regulation horseshoe like the ones the Raiders played with. On the way home from our malts, Hayley had had an idea and pulled in at the Wattses' mailbox and parked by the rail fence outside their barn, where three thoroughbreds in the paddock tugged at hay in a steel feeder. Florence Watts waved from the dark maw of the barn door. A thick gray braid hung from under a bandanna tied around her head, and she took off leather work gloves as she came toward us. I liked her. She was an old woman, not like Marie, but thin the way a knife blade is thin. Not powdery at all. She was sharp, still agile, and had a quickness about her. That was something I noticed: People who always seemed to do the right thing, by their own lights, had a certain verve. Florence was like that.

"Hey!" she said. "Did you two make some syrup? Geordie ran through the orchard the other day and said steam was coming out every opening of the cabin, just like those cartoons when someone gets really mad."

"Yes!" I yelled. "We're going to have pancakes for dinner!"

"How decadent."

Hayley said, "Florence, do you have any old horseshoes?"

"Heaps and heaps. I'm positively drowning in them. Come on."

In a corner of the tack room was a stack of what must have been sixty rusted horseshoes. Some still sported bent square-headed nails. "You can have them all. I don't know why on earth I keep them."

"Good luck," I suggested. This wasn't my first rodeo.

"Exactly, Frith! I think that must be why."

"Pick out eight, Pup," Hayley said. And I did. Eight of the least rusty, and the thickest—some had been worn down to nearly paper thin. We thanked Florence and continued on up West Hill.

So I was playing our own version of horseshoes when Rosie came up the track. I stood about ten feet back and threw them at the stick. Sometimes one hit and caught and circled around the stake. "Ringer!" Hayley would cry.

"Why do you say that?"

"That's what it's called. If you have a real metal stake it rings. It's the sound of winning. We'll get one, you'll see."

"Oh," I said.

Bear was barking this time as Rosie approached, not in alarm but with pleasure. "Horseshoes!" Rosie said.

"Wanna play?"

"Definitely."

"They're noncompliant," I said. Everything about us pretty much was.

"Great." Rosie scooped up four of the shoes like a pro. The red ones; we'd marked four with fire-engine-red nail polish. "You throw first," she said. "Home rules." And it really was home rules, because I have found out since that the true game is played with just two unmarked horseshoes and players standing at opposite ends of the pit. But that isn't nearly as congenial. And Rosie, who surely knew, never corrected me.

And that was the segue, how Rosie slipped into our lives, without having to make apologies or offer bribes. She simply picked up four noncompliant horseshoes marked with nail polish. I was relieved. I think Hayley was too. They'd finished the weekly six of beer yesterday, so Hayley brought out cold water in jelly jar glasses and we played horseshoes until the sun went over the ridge behind us and left a cold bruise over the trees.

*

So now a blizzard. I breathe myself to a certain calm at the big desk, let my hands rest on the pile of Hayley's old poems.

Here, in Northampton, it's very dark for two o'clock in the afternoon. The storm is not abating and seems more fierce. Can that be another inch of snow blown against the doors in however many minutes of musing? Probably.

Classes will be canceled tomorrow, I have no doubt. Amherst is conservative that way. Good. The prospect of students, of facing their bottomless need, is unappetizing to say the least. My 9:00 a.m. class is a seminar on sense of place in modern Latin American fiction. It's wildly popular, always way oversubscribed for the twelve coveted spots, and I teach it only because I want to read Mutis, Aira, Borges. It's usually fun—the fireworks of intellectual engagement, the crackle and pop of firing neurons, the excited hands being raised, the shy ones unable to contain themselves, the arrogant running headlong into their own limitations, my own love of sharing the work. Still, there is always beneath it this unmeetable hunger, this sense that I can never give these kids what they so badly need on some cellular, or spiritual, level. Neither I nor these magnificent authors can supply it. I wonder if pastors feel this way. I can inspire their best papers, give them A's even, and they will walk away just a little more diminished somehow. Not diminished, maybe, but unsure what they had come for or witnessed, like the Three Magi in Eliot's poem. They will walk into their adulthoods carrying these trophies as well as a scent of unnameable disappointment.

It was one of my heartbreaks. And I realize, pressing my eyes into the forearm of my sweater—a sweater that Rosie made for me before her death—that there is heartbreak at every turn, which is exactly what Li Xue was trying to tell us.

I lay the orchard poem upside down on a bare patch of blotter and slide the next poem toward me. I reach up and pull the chain on the standing lamp and read:

When I First Saw You

When I first saw you
there was still snow on Mount Tai.
We were so young!
The willows tossed their buds along the river.
You moved with the grace of a heron stalking the bank.

You hadn't married. Who needs a coarse man? you said.
My husband had been sent to the western wars.
Every night I went to the gate and hid my face in my sleeves.
Around me even the young locusts were singing for a lover.

You brought wine and we sang the "Boat Sailing Home"
song.
Overhead, waves of geese flew north.

Their barks fell out of the dark. Later, one came after, calling
and calling.
It's good to have a friend, you said, and poured another cup.

It's good to have a friend. It was good. The two of us, Hayley and I, newly arrived in town—well, a year before. In Vermont, newly arrived pretty much means anything less than three generations. It was good to have a friend in this strange, hard, beautiful valley. Why had she come? The question had still not been posed. *Who the fuck are you?* had never been followed by *Why the fuck are you here?* Which seems strange now. Maybe after a few days it was too late to ask. It was simply good to have Rosie around. Why queer a good thing?

And that too: Was she gay or bi? I honestly never knew. It didn't occur to me as a child, of course. And if I saw them sometimes holding hands side by side on the porch, well, Rosie held my hand too. Later, when I asked Rosie to reconstruct her conversation with Ivy next door, the one who had first piqued her curiosity about us, I took it at face value: There was an interesting, cultured, literate woman and her child who had just moved next door. They were eccentric in what seemed to be their chosen poverty; intriguing. In a rural village like Putney, that would be enough, wouldn't it?

Maybe. I never pushed the question because I guess I didn't want to know. I assume there are infinite and fluid territories along the spectrum of closeness, friendship, and love. Why try to set a hard border where there isn't any? We loved her. I loved her. There is a place for such naming in science, but in the messy taxonomy of love, there are too many hybrids, too many wild, one-off beasts. Thank God.

Whenever she came wafting up the dirt track, I saw the swatch of color first—of whatever homespun garment she was wearing. Then the bouncing, shining curls. Then I heard the voice, whether singing or humming or calling out. She never drove the final two hundred yards up the steep track, though she could have in her Forester. And then she would see me, and I would make out the frameless glasses, the light glancing off them, the lake-water blue of her eyes.

It was late March when we were playing horseshoes, almost April, and the sun had gone down over the ridge and a tide of cold flowed down off Putney Mountain. A dog barked in the distance over toward Grafton, and a coyote answered. Two coyotes, a moil of pitched howls and yips. We'd been hearing more of them lately. Overhead, dense clouds moved in masses toward the embered smudge of sunset as if heading into battle. Rosie threw her horseshoe with intense concentration; she didn't pull any punches playing with a seven-year-old. She made two ringers out of four. I made one. Granted, the stakes were maybe twelve feet apart, which, with her long arms, it seemed she could almost span.

"You're good!" I said, trying to sound more cheerful than I felt. I really wanted to win. I also adored playing someone other than Hayley.

"Closet redneck," she said. Whatever that meant.

Hayley called from the porch, "What's the score?"

"Nine to four," I said. "She's kicking my ass!"

"Frith! Jesus. Where do you get this stuff? Brrr. I made chili. You guys wanna eat?"

Rosie looked at me, raised an eyebrow, held out her hands, which clutched two horseshoes apiece. "Yep, okay," I said. "You wins."

"Wins?"

"That's how we say it. From when I was little and cute."

"Got it."

We lay the horseshoes by the near stake and walked up the short slope. Rosie put her hand on my shoulder, which I liked. She said, "A ringer isn't really a ringer without the ring, is it?"

"Nope," I said. Something about walking with her strong hand on me, with the air growing cold and the day going to dusk, and the distant coyotes and Hayley on the porch, and agreeing about this important thing—I felt happy. Safe. I felt I would burst.

*

The iPhone facedown at the far-right corner of my desk hums and emits a brave little hunting horn blast, called whimsically by its designer "Sherwood Forest." Hats off to them, the designer dudes and dudettes; it's the only thing I really like about the miraculous device.

The horn blast means I have a text. I reach for the phone, switch it to vibrate. Putting it at the far corner of the desk is a perfect geographical representation of my feelings for the thing. It's a text from Willum in the English department saying classes tomorrow are canceled. Why they let us know department by department is beyond me. Why can't a universal text go out to all employees, like an Amber Alert? It's not like, say, the School of Forestry is tougher than the rest of us and will take their pickups in to campus. Willum's text must not be to the entire department, because on mine there is an emoji. Two hearts, flying upward.

Willum.

The boy has a crush on me, he's made no secret. Can I say that anymore? Crush? Probably not. That's old-school. It's too sweet, too innocent. Charming. How can charm, of all things, lose its currency? Now I probably have to say that he wants to hook up. Everything reduced to its transactional essence. Well, the progress of history seems to be the extinction of nuance. In Victorian times, the sight of a bare ankle might give a man a boner, go figure.

Willum's a metrosexual from Illinois (his words) who has told me that he gets a complete body wax once a month. He eats his sandwiches with a knife and fork. He blushes when I enter the department office and the blotchy red goes down into his open shirt collar. He likes snap-front, yoked, plaid westerns that fit his slender body like a sheath. Also snug Hawaiians with volcanoes and hula girls. He talks with what might be called a feminine affect. Once, handing me my department mail, he tossed his soft blond bangs out of his face and blinked the long lashes of his chocolate-brown eyes and whispered, "Don't be fooled."

I stopped, turned around. "Don't be fooled by what, Willum?"

Husky whisper: "I'm as straight as an Apache arrow."

It's hard to stun me to silence. When my faculties of speech returned, I said, "Come again?"

Bad choice of words, maybe. He smiled shyly and flushed the color of a pomegranate all the way down to his hairless chest. We stared at each other. Maybe I was blushing too. Neither of us had anything to add, and after an endless moment he waggled his right hand in the surfer's hang loose sign and his smile got bigger and that was that.

On a warm Friday last October, I was leaving the building and I stuck my head in the office and he was alone there at the low counter, which I always call Prisoner Intake, and I asked him if he wanted to go out for a quick drink. "Well, duh!" he said and grabbed his fine leather flight jacket. We went to Sally's in Amherst, a forty-year-old pub that has allowed itself to be reincarnated through a perfect wheel of drinking-establishment suffering: biker blues club to fern bar to coffeehouse/wine bar to what it is now, a brewpub and tapas restaurant with vegan options. We know all this because the history is proudly displayed in photographs on the hand-plastered walls. It would be dizzying but for the fact that the place never changed its name. Also, the original DNA seems to be intact, because it still and always smells like old beer.

I am thirty-four, the same age Hayley was when she moved with me to the orchard. I am nearly as old as this brewpub. Who knew how old the water-smooth Willum was—old enough to drink, apparently, because the waitress palmed his driver's license as if she were reading her hand in blackjack and passed it back satisfied—but taking him to Sally's may have been a subconscious message on my part, the exact wording of which I cannot decipher.

As we slid into a booth I said, "How—"

He held up a hand. "Twenty-five. And three-quarters."

The beers were named after rivers, and I ordered the Blackwater Stout and he the Deerfield Wheat. Maybe it was because neither of us had eaten since breakfast, but within an hour I discovered that I couldn't name an author he hadn't read and we were both hammered.

*

I was talking about safety. The feeling of being safe as Rosie and I finished our game of horseshoes and walked up to the cabin. Hayley on the porch. Rosie's hand on my shoulder. The smell of stewed beef and chiles and woodsmoke. The flow of cold air down the mountain and the certainty that soon the night would freeze and the wet runnels between the tufts of new grass would glaze to thin glass that would crackle under my footsteps in the early morning. The opening of my heart and the release, like the song of a night bird, of joy.

Does joy require some sense of safety? I'm not sure. It's not that my life with Hayley had been joyless—there were moments, almost daily. She had a profound appreciation of beauty, and she had an ingrained sense of fun that expressed itself when the pressures of survival lifted just a little.

Safety, the sense of it, came in fleeting, warm swaths, like sunlight sweeping over the hills. We felt safe, a little, when Oliver's gas tank was full. When we carried the thick paper bags of groceries into the cabin and set them on the table and began putting away our provisions for the week. (We always got paper bags, because we used them to start fires in the woodstove. We also took extra produce bags, to use as Saran Wrap for leftovers. It wasn't stealing; Hayley always laid the four or five extra on top of the cart at the checkout aisle.) We felt safe when we snuggled in the ratty armchair by the popping stove at night. We squeezed in so tightly we could barely turn the pages of the book we would read together. And Bear our Bernese mountain mutt kept guard, sleeping over our feet, groaning and snoring.

Safe. To be held. To be protected. To feel Hayley's chin on the top of my head, rubbing as she read the book. To feel her strong arms encircling. To feel the breath in her chest pressing my thin back. I would listen, feel, and try to keep my inhales steady and anticipate the moment our breaths would coincide. A quiet joy in all of it.

I guess with Rosie around, it felt like suddenly our team was a little stronger, and that gave us more breathing room for joy and everything else.

Five

The maple trees that spring ran hard through the first week of April. Ideal conditions: freezing nights and days warming to T-shirt weather by midafternoon. Sawyer Brook rushed loudly with snowmelt and made roaring cascades out of the granite ledges and potholes. By the end of March, the snow was gone in the woods except for some stubborn drifts in the deepest shade on the north sides of the hills. Hayley and I managed to gather and boil enough sap to make twenty gallons of Grade A Dark, which sounds a lot better if you say eighty quarts. We tried to sell eighteen gallons to Bill the Buyer, but he refused. Hayley's face fell; I thought she would cry. Her scarred hand lay on the edge of one of the old wooden apple boxes, which held six big cans.

"It's really good," she said. "We graded it."

"Yeah," I chimed. "Made by apple maidens!"

"Do you want a sample?" Hayley said. Her mouth was quivering.

Bill, to his credit, seemed suddenly bewildered by the pain he had caused. "No, no!" he blurted. "I'm sure, I'm sure it's excellent. Best quality." His Croatian accent got thicker when he was agitated. "What I'm saying is you get twice the money if you set up stand in front of library. You can charge thirty dollars each gallon. Nobody will bother you there. I have a folding table if you need."

He squinted at the eighteen cans and bit his lower lip and said, "Just one minute," and disappeared through the hanging plastic strip door into the back of the store. A minute later he came back with a burlap sack stuffed with beige plastic jugs and a sheet of gold stickers that said Grade A Dark and a funnel.

"Better this way," he said.

What a sweetie. Hayley almost cried with relief. We all moved into a back corner of the store, where there was a low counter for giving out samples, and I held the jugs and Bill poured and Hayley put on the stickers and cleaned up the drips with a wet rag. Fifty-six quart jugs and thirty-two little pints. Wow.

We borrowed his card table; he even gave us two pieces of poster board and a marker to make a sign. Hayley wrote out in big green letters: "Apple Maiden Orchards Maple Syrup, SALE! $15 a quart, 9 Bucks a pint." Spelling out the "Bucks" was my idea. Then I drew a maple tree and a bucket and the two of us carrying sap in pails. We set up in front of the library, where local craftspeople of all types often sold homegrown stuff and were never hassled—a nod, I guess, to the democratic grassroots culture of rural Vermont. Hayley stood me at the table in my Monday Best and we sold out in four hours. We were rich. We had over $600 in flattened bills. I marveled at their feel in my hand—they were not quite paper, not quite thin rags. We walked across to the general store and Hayley spent fifteen dollars on a bottle of New Zealand red wine, and we drove the table back to Bill and I gave him the bottle. He blinked down at me and his face tightened; he almost looked severe. I held out the bottle and his big hand reached to take it and then remained on the neck, his fingers two inches from mine. They were shaking, I could feel it through the bottle.

"Thank you," he said. He took a deep breath. "I can't." He knew how much work those eighteen gallons had cost us and how broke we always were. I kept holding up the bottle. Even at that age, I knew that he was struggling not to diminish our dignity. "So kind," he said.

Hayley said, "We want to, Bill. It makes us happy. Take it. Please." And he said, "Okay, okay, thank you." He took the wine and for a second laid his hand on my head. I'll never forget that touch. He had lost his family in that horrible Balkan war, and Hayley told me later that he'd had a little girl. And then he turned away and was gone through those awful hanging plastic strips that look like stricken seaweed.

*

Rosie showed up the next day, late afternoon, which seemed to be her appointed time, when the springlike warmth turned a little chilly. This time she walked up the track in jeans and a green fisherman's sweater. She was carrying a rucksack. Bear and I ran down to meet her.

The sweater had thick cabling down the front and smelled like sheep. "Did you make it?" I said.

"Nope, I bought this one in Ireland."

"Hayley and I read all about Helen Keller," I announced. "Hold on, stop right there." She did. I closed my eyes and passed my hand from the ribbed neck down the front to the ribbed bottom.

"What does it say?" Rosie asked.

"I can't tell," I said. "It's in Irish."

She burst out laughing. "Wow," she said. "Gaelic braille is really tough."

"Yes, it is!" I said. I agreed with Rosie every time, even though I didn't get half of what she said. She unshucked the rucksack and pulled loose the string at its top and pulled out two shiny steel stakes. "Look what I've got." At first I was confused. Were these weapons, like the Viking short swords the women warriors used? And then it clicked: horseshoes! I danced around. "C'mon!" I cried. "Let's play, let's play! Let's get rid of those stupid sticks!"

She'd also brought two sixes of Catamount and a twelve-pack of root beer. It was a sunny evening, and the first swallows were out, slicing up the sky in the long light, and we cracked open cans like we were rich and played marathon horseshoes until it was too dark to see the shiny new stakes.

The sound. That's what I remember: the clank of a shoe hitting. The resounding strike as the toe, the heart of it, clanged and caught and spun on the stake. The ring of a ringer. In the still evening the rings sounded over the pulse of the brook below, the intermittent whine of a distant chainsaw, the dartings of the swallows that made no peep but hunted high into the depthless blue and cut so low and close to us I thought we might collide. It was the carillon of contentment.

I don't know what happiness is. Something we seek and try to hold on to, and in the holding lose like water through fingers. In my own life, the happiness that sneaks up is the only true one. Lands on your shoulder like a surprised bird and takes off again. And I will not name it. I can name the laughter that rose into that evening, the clangs and my own cries as I rushed forward to measure the throws.

I'm closer! I wins!

You are not!

Am too! Look, I measured how you showed me!

Paw!

Two points!

Damn!

Cuss all you want!

I was pretty good. I beat Hayley, who threw like a girl. Sometimes I beat Rosie, who was an old pro, probably trained-up in some redneck part of her past, probably visiting her relatives in the South. She hummed as she focused and tossed, thumb on the toe, backflipping the shoe like a North Country Raider. Hayley picked up the shoes as if she were on her way to do something else and just happened to see them lying there with her nail polish all over them. She held them a little like they might bite her, and she tossed as if relieved to get rid of them. Occasionally she lucked out and hit, or even got a leaner, and I decided that she had zero future in competitive horseshoes. But I noticed that she hummed and laughed just as readily as Rosie, and seemed lighter, and more delighted, than I'd seen her in weeks. I began to coach her, to encourage her, even when she was playing against me.

Go, Mom! Look at the stake when you throw! Not over there! The stake is over here. I whistled. I'd just learned to really whistle, and I annoyed everyone by whistling all the time. *Hey, Hayley—over there!*

She lowered the shoe. A swallow zipped right by her head. Beyond it I could see the first bright star in the blue. Maybe a planet. She cocked her head and assessed me with some amazement.

"Are you coaching me, Pup?"

"Um, well, you really need some coaching, Mom."

"Damn," she said. I think now that her incredulity had to do with me growing up. My time as Pup was not infinite. She stood there laughing in the dusk, and it was a laughter that carried a freight of sadness. Or knowledge, which I'm coming to believe is the same thing.

Rosie stood on the level bench of new grass below the cabin, ready to referee any close calls, looking from one to the other as in a tennis match.

It's good to have a friend, Li Xue wrote. It was good. For both of us. All of us.

*

Am I smiling at my desk? In the lamplight now, with the blizzard raging, and school canceled, and the file of poems in front of me? Maybe. I feel like it. I look down at the next handwritten page.

Sailing to Hu

As a child I sailed with my father to Hu.
Clouds hid the moon and lightning forked over the mountains.
We sailed into the willow bank and tied up.
Thunder boomed and the storm churned the black river to
white.
Our little boat bumped against the trees.
You held me and sang the Spring Planting song.

In the morning the sky was as clean as a washed singlet.
We pushed out onto smooth water.
When we got to the docks at Hu you asked
where we might find the poet Weng Xi.
Word must have got around: He came running
waving his arms, singing, "How wonderful!"

"Come, come!" he cried. "You two will stay for a month!
We will drink so much wine
and make so many poems we will forget them all!"

How did she do that? The poet and my mother. I have read bad translations, and they don't touch the spirit in the same way at all.

I can see that my mother loved Li Xue because she wrote of beauty and heartbreak and friendship in equal measure, and touched them all with grace. Every time I read one of these poems, I am transported, and then when I settle back on my perch, I wonder why my life cannot be filled with these things in this way. Where have I gone wrong? The world of the poems is so immeasurably rich. Am I depleted, or is it the world? How on earth do I get from here to there?

I used to believe that in nature I would be saved. And I was, a little. I would go back to the cabin, spend days, weeks. Back to the scene of the crime, so to speak. In whatever season. I would make coffee on the woodstove, the same one, and listen to the hiss of applewood and the chortle of the water in the blackened pot about to boil and smell the smoky coffee and the exhalation of the old planks in the floor. I would hear, too, the logs of the walls that shifted and cricked as the day warmed. I'd sit on the porch in the evening, on the same wooden bench—I'd sit on Hayley's side—and watch the orchard lose the sun, and when the shadows were gone, I'd follow the flights of the swallows as they darted and veered over the old trees. Watch until I lost their shapes in the dark.

Were those swallows the great-grandchildren of the ones we used to watch? The three of us sitting, finally silent, on the same bench? Talked out, laughed out, Hayley humming maybe. Or the great-great-grandchildren of those swift acrobats? How long does a swallow live?

And if I was sitting on the bench and it was early summer, or late summer, or fall, I'd get up after a while and clap the screen door and find one of the sweaters Rosie had knit for me and I'd pull it on. I'd smell the oil in the wool and probably the smoke and fragrances of a hundred shared meals, and a whiff of someone's perfume, maybe mine, and I'd bang the screen again and go back out and sit until the Bull rose over the valley, pursued by Orion. I'd sit until my fingers grew stiff with cold.

Could it save me? No.

Did I feel the two of them on either side of me, as if I could touch them? Just about.

Now, in Northampton, it's dark outside, full dark, and the wind has died. I can see the thick flakes, dimly lit by the patio lamps, falling straight down. I'm not hungry, but a cup of tea would be nice. At this time of day, it would usually be some herbal, a floral blend, nothing caffeinated, but this evening I'll make Lapsang souchong, liquid smoke, what the heck. I have nothing to get up for in the morning, no classes, and I have a feeling I'll be up late anyway. I stand and feel the heaviness of the new cargo. Ten weeks is not that far along, but already I'm aware of the weight, which is not at all like an overlarge Thanksgiving dinner. A weight that is wholly novel. I know I shouldn't drink caffeine, but I think it probably wouldn't be a crime to make a cup of weak tea. But before I go to the kitchen, I reach down and pick up the next poem.

To the Tune of "Summer Hawthorn"

Beneath the blossoms of the hawthorn
on the path to the river
she has no idea what a sight she has become.
Or that a single flower has landed in the hair at her brow.
Her song enchants the warblers, but she is clueless—
she is swinging her basket and dreaming of her beau.
She reminds me of the snowy egret
who thinks she is invisible against the bamboo hedge.

Ha! Hayley, why did you choose that poem next? The one before was about a parent and a daughter and about friendship. Made sense. Who was this about? Me? Or Rosie? Or maybe yourself?

I push back the chair and make my way down the hall, flicking light switches as I go.

Six

A few days after Rosie brought up the metal stakes, Hayley and I drove back to her house in Westminster West. She promised on the Bible she'd be there. She actually brought one, a battered King James that she said she got in Methodist Sunday school. It had her name embossed in gold on the cover. I flipped through it, fascinated by the way the columns of small print looked on the page, and by the lined, mostly blank sheets in the back for Births, Deaths, Marriages, Baptisms. There were only a few entries. In Deaths there was a scrawl in pencil in a child's hand that said, "Nicholas Bothmer 5, Kilt by a Car."

"Who was he?" I asked.

"He was my friend. I remember him. He had one of those flattop haircuts and he looked confused and sleepy a lot. Like he was always trying to catch up with what was going on and trying to figure out how to feel about it. Like a new puppy. Maybe that's why he didn't see the car."

"He got run over?"

"In the parking lot. He walked behind a car as it backed up."

"Whoa."

"I know."

Under Marriages it just said, "Aunt Sylvie."

"Who was she?" I said. The sap had finally stopped running in the maples, and without the pressure of emptying the buckets, Hayley and I felt like we were on vacation. It was a warm afternoon and I'd beaten Rosie once at horseshoes and then we had sat on the edge of the porch with our legs swinging and looked through the binoculars she'd brought. It was hard for me to catch a bird. I kept closing one eye, I don't know why, but with Rosie telling me gently to look first just with my eyes, then bring the binocs up without shifting my gaze, finally I saw one. I rolled the focus knob back and forth and a plump bird with a perfect black cap and white cheek resolved herself into miraculous detail. I could see the shine in her tiny eye. I guess I cried out, because Rosie said, "What what? Did you see that chickadee?"

"Yep!" I didn't know a chickadee from a wood duck.

"Great!"

After birdwatching, I spread a blanket on the porch and lay on my stomach and flipped through the Bible.

Rosie said, "Aunt Sylvie is Mama's younger sister. She married a chicken farmer, and then she divorced him because she said he started to look and act like a chicken."

I sat up. "Did he?"

"Oh, yeah, for sure."

"How?"

"His eyes got all beady and his nose looked like a beak. And he kind of jerked his head all over the place."

"He did?"

"Unh-huh. And one day she saw his *feet.*"

"His *feet?*"

"He'd always worn socks to bed. But one night she caught him coming out of the shower and . . ." She shuddered. "It's too awful."

"What? What?"

"No, I can't. You're too young."

"I am not! Please! Please!"

"He had three toes!"

"Oh! On each foot?"

"Yep."

I was struck dumb. I'd never heard of anything so wonderful and hideous. After that I held up the Bible and Rosie swore on it. Hayley came outside and said, "Are you swearing in Rosie as chief justice?"

"Nope, she is swearing she will be at her house tomorrow when we come over. Barring an act of God."

"I see. And when are we going?"

"Tomorrow afternoon, 3:00 p.m. Ish," I said.

We went. We loaded up Bear in the open truck bed and drove down Tavern Hill. It was a warm afternoon, with fluffy clouds sailing along in happy regattas. The North Country Raiders were out in front with their red plastic cups and we waved and they waved and I said, "Hayley, stop. I wanna talk to them."

"You do?"

"Definitely."

"You think that's a good idea?"

"Hell yes."

She cocked her head and stared at me. I think she spent most of that year reassessing me, every day.

"Well, all right."

Hayley was nothing if not game. She cranked the wheel to the left and pulled into their muddy driveway. I had a plan. I was wearing my Monday Best, at my own insistence, and hiding in the folds of honeysuckle was my favorite horseshoe. Blue nail polish at the heel. The six or seven Raiders turned from their game and watched as if an albino deer had just wandered into their yard. We got out. I waved. They waved. They were all huge men in black leather jackets, except one who was about my size. One had a Mohawk and a long gray beard and bare arms with spiderwebs at the elbows. I hooked the horseshoe into the ribbon at my waist and held up the hem of my dress and hopped around the puddles. I turned back just in time to see Hayley smiling at the men and shrugging.

I held out my hand to Mr. Mohawk. "Frith," I said. "Pleased to meet ya."

He squinted like he was sighting down a rifle, then cracked a half smile and squatted down and shook. His hand was the size of a dog bowl. I can still see it in my mind's eye. On impulse, as he withdrew it, I held on and turned it flat and read the knuckles like a book. On each finger was a letter and they spelled F-U-C-K.

I sounded it out—*fuuuck*—and then put my hand to my mouth. "Oh!"

I heard a rumble like a truck dumping gravel and he started to laugh, and then he was coughing. He stood, and he was hacking. When he finally stopped, he wiped his eyes and smiled down at me. "Sorry," he said. "Three packs a day. Pleased to meet ya, Frith. Name's Grimm."

Hayley stood back. This was my show.

"I wanna show you something," I said. "We kinda copied you."

"Be my guest."

I nodded. I strode to the center of the horseshoe pit, halfway between ends. I unhooked the shoe from my belt, sighted on a stake, thumbed the toe, and threw. Underhand, with backspin. The little shoe, about a third the size of theirs, tumbled through the air in a smooth arc, descended like a duck and caught the stake with a sharp ring, spun around it twice, and dropped to the sand. I'll never forget the yell that went up from that yard. One dude threw his cup in the air and the amber beer turned gold in the sunlight and then all the Raiders threw their beers. Maybe it wasn't gold, but I remember it that way. Like sprays of gold coins.

*

We chatted with the Raiders for a couple of minutes before we headed out. Sci-Fi, he was the little one, knew where we lived. He'd grown up in Dummerston. He knew Ivy Darrow and Ed Gray, all of the old families on West Hill; he'd gone to school with their kids. Rosie told us later that he was picked on in school, and when he was a freshman at Brattleboro High a senior pantsed him on the soccer field. Pulled off his pants so he had to run to the locker room naked while everybody laughed. The senior was found the next day floating facedown in an eddy of the Connecticut River, his torso torn open by a twelve-gauge. There's no way to do precise ballistics on a shotgun—Sci-Fi's family didn't even own one—and he was never charged. But nobody between Springfield and Burlington messed with him after that.

After I made my throw, he brought over four shiny new shoes. Regulation size.

"Here," he said. "A pro like you." That's the way he talked, in funny, fractured phrases. His eyes were like that too, green and brown, painted in flowy sections like a multicolored marble. It scared me a little. "Try." He bobbed his chin forward like Chicken Man. I tried. The shoe was too heavy. I couldn't make it fly more than the length of a body. Sci-Fi held his hands open like he was beseeching the Force. "Ah well. Later, gator."

A few of the Raiders talked to Hayley and admired the truck. Bear, to his credit, stood in the bed and wagged his tail. I bet the buffet of smells was amazing. Hayley looked so little surrounded by those big dudes, like a child.

One guy wore a leather cowboy hat and said our truck was his first car, same year, green not red. He loved it until he flipped it into the West River.

"My cousin drowned," he said.

"Oh! I'm sorry," Hayley said.

He shrugged. "He was kinda an asshole. Stole my pot and my girl!" He laughed. I have to say, I liked the attitude around this place. Kind of easy come, easy go, with a lot of jollity.

We waved as we pulled out. They all had red cups in their hands again and they lifted them in a salute. I felt like a queen.

*

After that, going to visit Rosie was like cream on pie. The yellow house with the blue door looked just as pretty as it had before, but brighter, as it was now in full sun. The greenhouse was boisterous with green. Rosie stood on the stone stoop as we came up the long, sandy drive, which was crunchy with old pine needles. I hopped from the truck and ran up the steps and she lifted me and hugged me and her sweater smelled like sheep and hay and her neck like lavender.

We followed her inside and to the kitchen island, but this time the vast expanse of hardwood was not the desert of Palestine but the Mongolian steppe.

Hayley and I had just seen a National Geographic movie about Mongol falconers, in Brattleboro, in celebration of my winning the first-grade spring poetry contest. Even though I was a one-day-a-weeker, I was considered a ringer in all things poetic and compositional, as word had gotten out that my mother was a famous translator. It's not like I was the only one from a brainy family; the hills around Putney probably harbor more advanced degrees per capita than any place on earth. We were less than an hour from the academic vortex around Amherst and only two hours from Boston and Cambridge.

After seeing the movie about the Mongol hunters, my ambitions were totally torn between ascending to Viking royalty and being a mounted falconress on the steppe and living in a yurt. Then Hayley got *Genghis Khan: Conqueror of the World* out of the library and read aloud choice bits before I went to sleep. Maybe a big mistake. If before I wanted to raid and savage the poor Scots and Celts all along the coasts, now I really needed a shortbow and a little horse and a thousand cousins with whom to sweep down the hill and into a sleepy, unsuspecting Kyrgyz town at full gallop.

Growing up, sadly, seems to be mostly about *not* becoming a Mongol.

So we followed Rosie across the steppe and the Persian rugs to the island where Marie had led us before, and we sat at the stools and Rosie poured us homemade raspberry iced tea and served us cheese curds she had made herself on fresh-baked bread. Is it a wonder that I mostly feel inadequate in my present life? What on earth do I do with my time? Certainly I don't make cheese. I seduce boys, apparently—boys almost young enough to be my sons. One boy. Age difference nine years, but still.

"Where's Marie?" I said.

"Resting. She should be out later. She played piano for an hour this morning and she's recuperating."

"Can you play piano?"

"I try not to."

"Can I play piano?" The words just flew out. I addressed them to the impossibly elegant instrument that sat on its four legs in the corner, as glossy and glamorous as a show horse.

Rosie cocked her head, wondering at my initiative, I suppose, and why the idea hadn't occurred to her. "Aunt Marie's a very good teacher. She taught for years. We can ask her."

"Huh," I said.

I was feeling, I think, a certain uneasiness. Hayley and I had had to work hard for everything together. Every morsel, every inch. But this morning a band of warriors who maybe (probably, actually) shot at people had lifted their cups to me in a toast. Someone had just offered me the use of a grand piano. Life wasn't supposed to work like this. I felt exposed, as if Hayley and I were walking into strange new territory, where we'd have to triangulate from different peaks. It was thrilling and scary.

*

The little yellow house in back was a perfect replica of the big house, but scaled down. It had a front porch trimmed in white, with lathed newel-posts, and a gabled window upstairs with curtains of the same wild rose pattern. Why are miniatures, or scaled-down things, so fascinating? I guess one reason might be that, for a moment, we get the Gulliver effect. The smallness of the house or boat or guitar zooms us suddenly up in size and we can see our lives as if from a distance, from a certain height—we can take the long view for a minute and realize that everything is so neatly assembled and amazing. Maybe that's not it at all. Rosie's house wasn't a miniature; it wasn't a train set or a ship in a bottle, or even a playhouse. It was a house. It was just small, the little twin of the one beside it, and somehow that lent it some magic.

We carried our drinks in their tall glasses up the flagstone path. I had never carried a drink in a glass up a path, with rattling ice—we always had cans—and it made me feel ladylike. Rosie held open the screen door and we stepped inside.

The room was floored with the same heartwood, and in the middle of it sat a loom. It took up most of the space, and it had the same quality of quiet repose and poised exuberance as the piano. Like the piano, it was made mostly of wood, this time oak staves, and it was strung like an instrument; and like the piano, it had been left just as it was last touched, as the last note reverberated, so to speak. And so it seemed alive somehow, as if it contained some part of the life of the weaver and would leap into action at the first encouragement.

The more I looked at it, the more complicated a contraption it seemed, with frames and ropes and arms and levers, until I thought it looked less like an instrument than a torture device. In the library at school there was a book about the Spanish Inquisition, and I snuck it into the empty science lab and read it through with wonder-struck horror. I flipped through the illustrations, and there was one poor bearded heretic stretched out on something that looked a lot like this loom.

A soft light filtered through the white curtains, which stirred as the warm breeze came through the open windows. The room smelled of wool and the thawing earth outside. There was a stuffed armchair in the corner and a cot along one wall, covered in a woven blue blanket, and except for the loom, I thought the whole scene was like *Goodnight Moon*. I checked Rosie quickly to make sure she wasn't the grandmother.

"Here, this is what I'm working on now." Rosie led us to the loom, and stretched across the strings was a scene in blues and palest pinks, greens, light violet. It was hills, our hills, but in May, when all the woods were new and tender green, and there were the orchards, a checkerboard patchwork in full blossom. White, barely tinged with pink. The light suffusing them, without a doubt, was evening light. And there was our pond, I thought, and the river running through the valley, and descending down over the ridges on extended wings—overlarge, the perspective being from a camera above and behind him—flew a hawk with blood-colored shoulders and a barred tail. I shivered. I'd never seen a woven tapestry. It was beautiful and terrifying.

"What's he doing?" I murmured.

"He's hunting."

"He's hungry?"

"Sure. He's looking for dinner."

The hair stood up along my arms.

"Is that where our house is?" I pointed but didn't touch.

"I suppose it'd be right there."

The hawk seemed to be staring at the spot, dropping to it. I didn't look at her and I didn't say anything after that. My heart was racing.

"Come," Rosie said brightly. "I'll show you some of the possibly terrible sculptures."

Seven

I do not flick on the kitchen light. I can see well enough. I stand at the counter in the half dark and listen to the cessation of the wind. Cessation also has a certain sound which can be quite as loud as the noise which preceded it. Louder sometimes.

One night when Hayley was scribbling by the light of an Aladdin lamp—I still think the kerosene glow of an ash mantle is the prettiest indoor light on earth—I asked her what she was writing. She looked up all blurry as if out of a dream and said, "Oh, I'm writing silence, Pup. I'm trying to capture the thunder of it."

"Thunder?"

"Silence can sometimes be louder than thunder, don't you think?"

I thought. Hayley rubbed her eyes and said, "C'mon." She scraped back the chair and took my hand and we went out on the porch. Bear got excited and for a minute all we could hear was his breathing. "Lie down!" I said and tumped him, and he lay down against my legs and after a while his panting subsided. We listened. A heavy overcast lidded the hills, and the only light was thrown by the lamp through the window. We could hear rushing water, we could hear frogs, peepers, and one bullfrog thrumming from the pond. It was a June night and the grass was already tall under the apple trees and we could hear the wind running through it and rustling the leaves. The apples and the woods behind the cabin shirred in different tones.

"It's not silent at all, is it?"

"Nope. It's crowded," I said.

She squeezed my shoulder. "That's a good one. That's just what it's like. I might have to take you out west to hear real silence."

She placed her open hand on my head, and I could feel her traveling. "There can be a silence when someone says good-bye," she said. "But even then, you can hear your heart pounding. In your ears."

"So is that like thunder?"

She thought for a second and said, "Yes."

The silence now, in the kitchen, is the cessation of a storm wind, and there is such an absence of sound I might have thought this is what Hayley meant. Absence muffled by falling snow, which is really as quiet as it gets. But then I hear the patient tick of the wall clock and the hum of the refrigerator's compressor. And of course I cannot keep from hearing the low din, like its own compressor, of my own past.

*

I boil water for tea. I do it all by the light of the digital clock on the back of the stove. I scald the mug and pour the water over the bag of Lapsang souchong and smell instantly the smoky oils rising in the steam. I imagine outdoor fires in the hills of Assam, the snowy Himalaya rising in the distance. I sit on a stool at the butcher block island and wonder at my fear in Rosie's studio. I was only seven, but I was not immune to symbolism or artistic suggestion. Seeing the hills in the weaving, *our* hills, and the predatory bird flying over and seeming to target our home—it scared me deeply. In a way that dovetailed with my uneasiness in Rosie's kitchen. Did the vantage of the viewer, and the weaver—just behind the eyes of the hawk—suggest that Rosie was the raptor? I might not have had these words, but I had the intuition. If Rosie was the raptor, then she was a predator and she was hunting our hills, if not our very house. So then the disquiet I'd felt looking at the piano, the bookshelves full of art books, was the alarm any child should feel in any story or fairy tale when things are too shiny and come too easily. You can get stuffed in an oven or a kettle or the beak of a giant bird.

Maybe that's what Rosie saw that afternoon: my fear. I remember how she turned toward the far end of the studio, then turned back. "What's the matter, Frith?" she asked. I was still fixated on the weaving on the loom. I felt her large hand on the top of my head and I started. Her hand cupped my head like a talon.

"I, uh . . ."

"Do you like it? It's a blanket, I'm making it for you. I probably shouldn't have told you! I know how much you love birds."

My mouth opened and no sound came out. "She's speechless," Hayley said, and pulled me into her, to her side, out of Rosie's grasp. Rescue.

I summoned all my courage and straightened and stepped away from Hayley's skirts. "Why is he hunting over our cabin?" I said.

Rosie cocked her head and looked down at me and I saw the white curtains moving in her rimless glasses and the blue eyes behind them, which I had to admit were kind. "Actually," she said softly, "I think it's a she. Maybe she's protecting you."

Rosie led us through the small door into the rest of the studio.

*

I let the tea steep, not for long. I am never patient enough to let it sit in the cup for the full three minutes recommended on the box—who does that? Anyway, it should probably be weak. I squeeze the bag—another no-no—and set it in a mini ceramic bowl with a blue pattern, the kind used for soy sauce in sushi restaurants. The blue enamel design is an arching catfish. I am not supposed to drink caffeine while pregnant, according to Dr. Liu, my obstetrician. She said at my last exam that there are a million things one is not supposed to do, and that with the exception of the truly egregious stuff like smoking and drinking and doing drugs, and maybe UFC cage fighting, in her estimation doing things that make one happy—in moderation—is probably okay, because being a happy expectant mother is more important than almost anything. True for life in general, she said. And so when one of her patients wants to cross-country ski-race up to two months before her due date, she gives her a thumbs-up.

I told her that my mother, Hayley, admitted to me that she drank coffee, beer, and bourbon, and occasionally smoked, during her pregnancy with me. Hayley said, "Pup, given how you turned out, I have zero regrets. Think what a genius you might be if I'd indulged more!" That's the way logic worked in our little family. Dr. Liu's raised eyebrow, neatly plucked, expressed her disapproval, both of Mom's behavior and of her reasoning. I studied my doctor: She was, I thought, an excellent obstetrician—caring, off-the-charts smart in all things medical, patient, clear in her explanations, efficient, well organized, and intelligent enough to keep things simple. (Smarts and intelligence being two different things in my book.) She was compassionate and she had a sense of humor. With her bobbed black hair and neat black eyebrows and snow-white coat, her oval face and symmetrical features, she was also very attractive. Maybe it was the last poem that made me think of her, the one about the snowy egret against bamboo.

I had looked at her typing notes into a laptop and wondered at all the ways to approach a chaotic universe, an earth of surpassing beauty, a life of constant loss.

Here was one way. Helen Liu. Who had clearly studied extremely hard and learned efficiencies of thought and emotion that were truly admirable. It was not that she saw the world in black-and-white, I thought, but there was a clean line running through her life, an obviously right way to do things. With information ordered correctly and correctly tested, there would always be clear conclusions on how to proceed. And if the conclusions sometimes were not all that clear, there would at least be a reasonable statistical assessment. And the chips would fall, and one would sleep at night knowing one had done the very best one could.

I saw all this in the efficiency of her movements and the ease of her smile, in the clear way she expressed everything. She was not wasting a ton of energy on regret or second-guessing. Why would she?

Helen Liu awed me. I would not deny her the humanity of feeling sometimes as hurt or confused as any of us. Or lonely, or angry, or empty. Of course she did. But I imagined that she would not be at a complete loss. She would have a certain perspective, the way devout religious people do, that would help her put those emotions in the proper place, a place where she might have some peace with them—and then move on. And so she would be, probably was, the most wonderful mother and wife—because though she worked very hard, more of her emotional energy would be freed up and generous.

Wow. Way to have this life by the short hairs, as Rosie used to say. This was how I imagined Dr. Liu. Now imagine me, dear Frith, and all those of my ilk.

There is no way to correctly order all the information, all the stimuli, every minute, because the imagination is running wild, always traveling, and introducing new trajectories of inquiry, new spoilers, new territories, new fairies and new monsters. In the cacophony of birdcall and voices there is really no way to properly order anything. We do the best we can, but. The Cheshire cat smiles down on us and a rabbit hole opens. So we follow our noses, our curiosity, our impulses, and our loves, and our lives are generally a mess.

And so of course we are heartbroken half the time, and half the time at a loss, and half the time wondering why we took *that* path, and half the time humming and excited as we explore some new trail, which all adds up to way more than 100 percent, which is part of our problem.

Introducing Hayley, introducing Frith. The noncompliant apple falls really close to the tree.

What Hayley did to find a through line was to have me. And to translate some of the most beautiful lines ever written. Because she continued to work on the poems at the orchard. In the beginning she was shy about it, even with me, I don't know why. She'd pull out the Chinese texts at night when she thought I was asleep. But the cabin has a sleeping loft in the back, still does, a simple platform eight feet up, accessed by a ladder. I would worm over to Hayley's side of the bed, the main-room side, and hang my chin over the edge of the mattress and watch her work at the table from above. She worked by the light of the kerosene lantern and it suffused her loose hair in a soft nimbus and when, in a gesture that was wholly unconscious, she shoved the strands behind her ear, it cast an unforgiving light on the plane of her sunspotted cheek, the crow's-feet at the corner of her eye, the back of her hand as she wrote. Her hands were scarred and tanned nearly black.

A person seen from above, head bent, unsuspecting, can seem very vulnerable. I could see the jagged part in her hair, like a careless path between untended fields. The scalp exposed there was tender and pink, because the part never fell in the same place and so would not get tan. I could see grass seeds stuck between strands, even one white hair in all that auburn, which shocked me.

She slid the Chinese texts toward her from a small stack: clean sheets with vertical rows of characters, sometimes in calligraphy. Clipped to the sheet was a page of literal translation, character by character, just words and phrases, and at the bottom was a paragraph of her interpreter's sense of the meaning in English, with possible alternate phrasing. This was followed by any notes on context the interpreter deemed germane. On the table, on her right, was a thick Chinese-English dictionary, and beside it a small stack of volumes in translation of poetry by Li Xue's contemporaries or near contemporaries. These included Li Bai, Du Fu, Wang Wei, and also the women Xue Tao, Yu Xuanji, and Li Ye.

Hayley couldn't speak Chinese or read it all that well, but she had a familiarity with the characters and deep knowledge of both the antecedents of Li Xue's poetry and the poems of those working in her lifetime. She was also well-read in the cultural and historical contexts of the time, which was a period of religious transition and political upheaval.

One didn't need to know the source language, apparently, to be a brilliant translator. Hayley told me that in her estimation the poets Kenneth Rexroth and W. S. Merwin were hands down the greatest translators of the Tang, and to her knowledge neither one could order properly in a Sichuan restaurant.

That was my cue. "You order," I cried. "I'll be the waitress!"

We would be on the porch in the evening, sitting on the bench, which we moved back against the log wall, back in the shade, as the afternoons were getting warmer.

I'd run inside, banging the screen door on its spring, and find a stained white dish towel and wrap it around my waist like I'd seen the girls do at Dragon Princess, the Sichuan restaurant on Route 5, on the way into Brattleboro. We would always eat there on the last Sunday of the month, when they had dim sum, which Hayley explained to me was not at all Sichuan, but very popular with Americans, who mostly had no idea that the people in Guangzhou and Hong Kong didn't even speak the same language as people in, say, Chengdu.

I'd wrap and tie the towel; I'd corral my hair and pile it on my head and stick two pencils in it, the way the girls did with chopsticks, and I'd fold up a sheet of paper—there were always scrap paper and pencils and pens on our table—and grab a pen and take a deep breath and compose myself and come through the door. With a very serious expression I would say, "*Wo ke yi dian can ma?*" May I take your order? Hayley taught me.

"*Qing*," she would say. Please.

"*Wo ke yi le*," I would say. Ready.

"How are your short ribs?" she would say in English.

"Very extremely delicious."

"I'll take two orders." I'd raise an eyebrow and write it down.

"How is your twice-cooked pork?"

"Original and extremely satisfying."

"In that case, I'll have three orders, please."

We would go on like that until Hayley had ordered a Mount Tai of food, and then she would say, "That will be all for now, I guess. If I'm still hungry, I'll take a look at the menu again." And she would say, "*Xie xie*," and I would bow my head and say, "*Xie xie*," and hurry off.

I'd come back and say that I regretted that we were all sold out of this and that. Also, that the cook had had a heart attack but the doctors thought he would live, that the dog had sadly eaten all the ribs, and I'd put in front of her a bowl of cold, hard oatmeal from the morning. Or one of Bear's bones on a plate. There were endless variations. Once, on a Wednesday when I'd been to school, I begged her to play, and in the end I piled a plate with real chicken chow mein that they'd served us at school and that I'd smuggled home in my pack. I served it to her under a pot lid, and when she lifted it off warily, she laughed so hard I thought she might actually croak.

How did I get to that story? Her translations. She worked at night, sometimes very late. She would sound out the characters she knew, which were most of them, with the intonations she believed were correct, and she would let the music linger on her tongue. I loved that so much, listening to the words formed twelve hundred years ago roll from my mother's lips and flutter mothlike in the lantern light, and sink like snow to the floor. She uttered them quietly so as not to wake me. I never knew if she had any idea I was awake and listening. Maybe it was her way of singing me a lullaby. And then she would slide the sheet closer and study the transliterations word by word, sometimes intoning them in English. Which for me was like dessert. I squirmed forward and leaned my head down farther and strained to hear: *mist divided / bamboo / jade spring / flies / Tsu Mountain / lonely / temple bell / two pines / lean / sleepy / master Du Peng / no sign / few women / face / hide / two sleeves.*

"I'll be damned," she would say softly. "After Li Po. Almost plagiarized. Wait a sec . . ." Her running monologue. "Ahh, here we go. Suzanne's note says, 'Dedicated to dear friend Li Po after a surprise visit.' Okay, got it." I loved watching, listening to her work. She must have known, because I think that on many nights I fell asleep where I lay, sideways on the bed, enchanted with the show beneath me.

*

She must have planned to publish a second volume of Li Xue's work. I imagine it might have had a title like *The Orchard Poems.* When Li Xue left Chang'an as a prospective widow—despite numerous inquiries, she could get no definitive answer on her husband's whereabouts after the bitter Battle of Talas—she, too, moved to an orchard, in the hills above the Yellow River. She was young and very pregnant and heartbroken. And so I always thought that, in moving us from Denver to Putney, Hayley was recapitulating Li Xue's self-exile. Or salvation. And that in some way the mirroring of two lives, separated by so many centuries, might have been Hayley's way of getting so close to the world of the poems that her translations would be truer. I know now that she was that fully dedicated to her work, her art. Or maybe she just saw Li Xue as a model she had wanted to emulate her whole life.

I carry the cup of tea back to the desk. I shuffle through the notebook pages and find, three pages further in, the poem I remember her sounding out—a poem in the long tradition of visiting a master or friend and not finding them home.

Note Left for Master Du Peng
After Climbing Tsu Mountain and
Not Finding Him Anywhere

I have climbed Tsu Mountain to see you, old friend.
Bamboo stands out of cold mist.

Jade springs fly from wet cliffs.
It's so high and lonely the temple bell tolls as in a dream.
No one knows where you have gone.
Two pines lean together like sleepy friends.
I sit beneath them and write you this note.
Few women ever come this far
but you are the only one I wanted to talk to.

Did Hayley take the liberties it seems she took? Probably. A great translator always will. Because one who is too deferential "is running a railroad," Hayley once told me. "Shunting words together like boxcars."

"Got it," I said. What I'd got I had no clue, but I would never forget the figure of the train. She explained to me that every poem has a certain music, and that the sound of it is as important to the meaning as anything else. Does it sound hard and bright like a tinkling chime, does it rill along like a stream, or is it soft and sad like slow rain?

I loved watching her work, and the more I think about it, the more I believe she loved watching me watch her. I think it was a way of sharing her work with me and still allowing herself to be fully focused. She was giving the best of herself, directly to me, and at the same time giving me an education in poetry, in translation, in the creative process. Because when she would assemble the words and phrases and notes and sound out the lines over and over—drifting, I think, fully into the world of the poem—and then when she would finally recompose the lines in the voice of Li Xue, which had become her own voice, she would recite them aloud. I would close my eyes and I, too, would drift into the pine forest on Tsu Mountain on a cold and misty day.

We read a lot together—children's books like *Charlie and the Chocolate Factory,* and more advanced books like *Treasure Island,* and adult books that seemed perfectly pitched to my pugnacious sensibilities, like *We Die Alone,* about the Norwegian commando who outskied an entire Nazi division, and *Grendel,* by John Gardner. She also read to me a bunch of poetry, my favorites of which were "Archy and Mehitabel," about the cockroach and the cat, and e.e. cummings, and, believe it or not, W. B. Yeats. He wanted his daughter to grow up to be like a tree. A laurel tree. Which seemed to me to be pretty enlightened for a dad. My view on the poem and its patriarchal sentiments changed over time, but not my love of the music.

We read a lot, but I was never more immersed, more lost, than when I was hanging my chin off the edge of the bed and listening to ancient Chinese poems while looking at the top of my mother's head.

*

So, that day visiting Rosie in Westminster West: She turned toward the end of the room, away from the dropping hillside and the brook, which we could hear through the screens. At that end was a small door I hadn't noticed, smaller than it needed to be even in this little house, and painted the same color as the pale yellow walls. I guess, given our literary sensibilities, it's not surprising that in the little yellow doll's house of

Rosie's studio I began to wonder if I were entering a fairy tale and so got spooked. Especially as we ducked through a door that was too small. Or they ducked; I walked right through.

The ceiling beyond the door was for some reason a couple of feet shorter, and Rosie's thick blond hair nearly brushed the paneling. The room itself was not small in width or length, which was remarkable, as the cottage seemed so diminutive from outside. The walls were covered with weavings. Not an inch of space remained. Hayley and I had been to the art museum in Brattleboro a bunch of times. It was free. This was like a gallery room except way more crowded, and the hangings were like paintings in the precision of detail where they wanted to be precise, and in the washing of color and form where they wanted to be washed. But they were also three-dimensional and they tufted out in bursts, or were lumpy right across, or riven with canyons, or striped with logs, or rippled like hay fields pressed and smoothed by wind and sun. They were mostly landscapes. I must have gasped or cried out. I know that all my fear had flown, and when I glanced up, Rosie was peering at me quizzically.

"Cool?" she said.

"Cool!" I said.

I went right to the wall and reached out to touch and stopped, and I heard Rosie say, "It's okay, that's what they're made for."

My hand passed over the ground, the forest, as a cloud's shadow would pass over. I felt wool or cotton or silk, warm and neutral and almost cool. My palm brushed tufty treetops, tickling grassheads, smooth water. And the place, the truth of it, its temperature, or voice, or essence, somehow traveled through the hypersensitive skin of my open hand and right up through my arm and into my chest. I hesitate to say heart, because I don't want to diminish the profundity of the sensation by sounding corny. Whatever it did, it was remarkable. It did what listening to Hayley did as she sounded out poems at night—the sense of immersion and transport—but here it was all at once in the immediacy of touch.

I can say that I have felt almost the same thing with boys, but only two.

All thoughts of Rosie as some witch were banished. "Is that a herd of zebra?" I said after feeling their stripes.

"I guess it could be."

"What do you think it is?"

"I think it's a herd of horses in a faraway land striped by the shadows of aspen trees."

"Not tigers?"

"Well. What do they feel like?" I felt again. It was a smaller weaving, maybe only two feet by two feet, and as I think about it now, it was nearly abstract. But I got animals and I felt the presence of trees.

"They feel like tigers who would like to meet a bunch of horses striped by tree shadows."

"Then they could sneak up on them?"

"Yep."

"How about this one?" Rosie said. She led me to the far wall and gestured at a large hanging of chaotic blues and blacks and dashes of white and two birds rising and turning off sharply. "Waves!" I said. I could feel their power. And the speed of the sleek birds, their impossibly wide wings.

"Yep. It's the Southern Ocean, near Antarctica. In a storm. Those are albatross."

"Wow."

"I was with this group called Sea Shepherd for two years. When I was in my twenties. We went down there in an all-black pirate ship."

"You did?"

Rosie nodded. My estimation of her was growing by the minute.

A few of the other pieces I remember: a remarkable weaving of waterfalls in the course of a dark green brook, and one of a tree holding boats in its branches like large fruit, and a Chinese pagoda beneath a snowy mountain, with a nude woman lying in the foreground as if the scene behind her were a dream. The pagoda was warm to the touch and the mountain almost cold and the woman was cool. I have thought about that often since. Of course, it must have been the choice of thread or sewn fabric—every material and cloth has its own temperature—but it still seems magical.

We went back through the undersize door into the bright airiness of her weaving room and then into the windy cool of the afternoon.

"Why was the lady lying in front of the house?" I said. I wouldn't have thought to ask why she was nude. Hayley and I spent half our lives naked.

"I'm not sure, but I think she's waiting for something."

"For what?"

"For something to change."

That made an impression on me too—something I would turn over in my mind many times: that the artist doesn't have to know anything about her work and usually doesn't.

We came through the back door and found Marie in the center of the room, again wearing all white and cream, again very powdery and leaning on her cane. "The baby's hungry," she said in her soft way. Sitting beside her, head inches from her knees like a dog in a portrait, was Bear. He had a lace baby bonnet tied to his head with a silk ribbon. It sat between his ears at a rakish angle. I'd forgotten all about him.

*

"She's got some dementia," Hayley said in the truck on the way home.

Rosie had insisted on feeding us, and by the time we'd driven back it was dark. Between newly budded branches, bright stars skimmed through wind-driven clouds. We were the only ones on the Westminster West Road and Hayley turned off the lights, which she did sometimes when she wanted the stars to be brighter and the night closer. It was deliciously cold, and we drove with the windows cranked down and the wind pouring over us. I felt inexplicably happy. Again. This could get to be a habit. It had something to do with the successive waves of fear and relief I'd experienced all afternoon. I'd never really been to anyone else's house, and I was learning that it could be invigorating, bracing. But now it was just Hayley and me again, on our own, and Bear in the back, sans bonnet. We were full of good food—we'd had bread pudding and ice cream for dessert—and we were a team, all three of us. And other people were mostly crazy or at least odd.

Dementia. I sounded it out. "Demented!" I said.

"Right." We passed the llama field on our right, and I could see spots of luminescence on the hillside, which must have been the patchy llamas. We passed a farmhouse with a single fake candle alight in every window.

"Why do they do that?" I said.

"The candles?" Hayley said.

"Uh-huh."

“For fun, I guess.”

“Whoa.”

“It’s not that Marie’s crazy,” Hayley said.

“What is she?” I said.

“She’s mixed up. It happens sometimes when people get old.”

“Oh.”

After that we were quiet and let the thump of the tires and the chirping springs and rattling windows do the talking.

Eight

I own the blanket of the orchard-quilted hills and the red-shouldered hawk flying over. I know it's a redshoulder because Rosie gave me my first set of binoculars and a Sibley's bird guide and began to teach me my birds. The weaving is one of my very few prized possessions. That and the set of eight real horseshoes painted with blue and red nail polish. And Hayley's stack of poetry books from the Tang. And this chest, which I could not open for so many years.

I don't sleep under the blanket, and neither can I hang it. It's large for the cabin, five by four. I nailed up the eight shoes, one on top of the other, to the right of the door as you're going out. Heels up, of course, for good luck. The blue-painted ones are on top, Hayley's color. But the blanket I could not display, I'm not sure why. The intention was so good. When I looked at it closely a second time, I could see that the raptor was not hunting but was indeed flying over our country with a benevolent, protecting spirit.

But some things can't be protected against—with art, or gifts, or prayers.

The morning after we went to Rosie's, I woke up to an empty bed. Sunlight blazed my face from the one high, canted window over the door. It dazzled my eyelids and I turned over and Hayley was not spooning me. I was always the first to wriggle out of bed, out from her arms. It's the reverse, I know, from how most households work, with the kids having to be prodded to wake up, but we weren't most households. Hayley worked hard during the day at whatever the current scheme was for our survival, and she read and translated late into the night. How late I never knew, because I dropped off. But this morning I woke to an empty bed. I shucked my nightie and pulled on shorts and a sweater and clambered down and out the door.

She was sitting on the porch in the level bore of a sun rising over the New Hampshire hills across the river. She held a steaming mug in two hands and her eyes were closed—against the sun or whatever thoughts. She heard the spring of the screen door and she moved her lips. "Hi, Pup," she whispered without opening her eyes.

"Are you meditating like Buddha?" I said.

She shook her head.

"What are you doing?"

"I had a bad dream," she said.

"Oh." Usually—no, always—I knew right where to go all the time. Now I didn't. I stood on the porch. "Do you want an egg?" I said. She smiled a little and shook her head.

"What was it about?"

Her mouth quivered and she said, "Your dad died last night. Ivy just stopped by late."

*

Hayley had told me often, since I was really little, that she loved my father very much, that he was a good man, but that he was sick in a way that could unintentionally harm others and we couldn't be around him. She left him when I was three, and I don't remember anything of him except, oddly, a laugh. A laugh and a swoosh, as he swooped me up, maybe, and a blur of blue bandanna. A laugh that always seemed in a different accent than English, though I'm not sure how that could be. But I was right, because Hayley said Pop spoke Cajun French; he was from a crawfishing family near Jeanerette, Louisiana. She said he would scoop me up, laughing, and say "*Cagou! Chère-petite!*" I don't know if I put the accent on his laugh later, when I knew all this. It wasn't until we left Denver that she explained that he was a heroin addict. She told me that it was a disease and that one of its symptoms was that he became crazy and did hurtful things that he would never, ever do had he been free of it. That was why we couldn't be around him even though we loved him very much.

That morning she'd been crying. I could see the salty tracks of her tears. And remembering that, I am struck again by the concurrence and sympathy with Li Xue. The Tang dynasty poet had lost her husband at a young age, to battle. And so had Hayley. To a type of war that had ravaged her husband and taken him far away, even years before his death.

But death, the real death, is permanent, as Li Xue had said in the poem titled "The Orchard." And so maybe, like the poet, Hayley had harbored a hope that Johnny Cormier would one day free himself and return.

Now he wouldn't, ever. Standing on the porch, I felt a surge of grief too; not for him or myself but for my mother. I hated to see her sad. So I turned around and went back inside and made her a cup of tea, just like the one I'm drinking now. Tea was a luxury back then. Coffee a necessity, as necessary maybe as air, but tea was something she indulged in, and I boiled the water and scalded the cup, as she taught me, and let it steep and added cream and honey and brought it to her, and sat with her on the bench while she cried.

*

Now, in Northampton, I pick up the mug of my own tea and inhale the smoky steam and look down at the thin stack of papers. The next poem—I had an idea what it would be about, and it is.

On Confirmation of the Death of My Husband

The letter arrived today, by messenger from Chang'an.
Words of condolence, apologies for the long delay.
A wooden box with your seal inside.

Who cares?
The maple leaves are falling. I pull at my hair.
Overnight I have become an old woman.
Cranes fly south bleating in the dark.
In spring they will fly back and you will still be gone.

And another, maybe a rewrite of the first.

When you left, you were just a boy.
Riding proudly behind the banners of Chang'an.
Today the messenger handed me a little box containing
your seal.
The box might as well be your tomb. I look inside
searching for life, your scent—nothing remains.
Our infant daughter plays on the floor.
Her laughter echoes against the cliffs of my silence.
Outside a loon wails and wails in the dark.

And another.

After Li Po and Li Shangyin

The moon doesn't keep track of how many cups I drink.
She bobs along on the river of stars unconcerned with my sorrow.
I once had a beau whose voice touched me like falling blossoms.
We were just kids and we couldn't wait to make a life together.
We got married and the moon sailed behind us.
What happened? If you came through the gate this evening
I would tell you how the nights have gone silent without your
laughter.
I will never again hear the sound of your horse clapping up
the road.

I want so much to tell you how I remember you tonight—
you are my first and only love.

It will have to wait until we meet again on the far side of
Star River.
Until then, let's not forget each other.

I almost wonder if Hayley wrote these herself. I could do the research but won't. It doesn't matter. Who cares? as Li Xue possibly said. The two women, across twelve centuries, were going through similar loss and sharing the language.

Reading now, I feel close to them, but not part of the sisterhood. I am going through something else—the prospect of raising a child alone—but it's not the same. Not the same as widowhood. If Willum, God forbid, overdosed on Molly, or whatever party drug is the thing these days, and died—would I write poems like these? I mean, if I *could* write poems like these?

No. I'd be sad. I'd think, *What a waste.* I'd think that my daughter (I don't know the gender yet, of course, but I am almost certain she's a girl) will never have a living mystery father to track down. Well, if she has the research chops of her mother and grandmother, she would find him anyway, perhaps visit his grave with flowers on Father's Day. This is as baroque as I will get on the subject, but you can see that my heart is not broken and never will be.

And maybe that's what I envy about these women. That they could love that deeply. Could I? Did I? Did I call my own mother Hayley because I never wanted to be that vulnerable? I shiver. And not from the cold or the blizzard, which enacts its deathly beauty outside, behind double panes of glass.

*

It was fun, my tussle with Willum. We had drinks at Sally's, vodka and cranberry juice, go figure. We both had the same, which was some tacit acknowledgment that we weren't there for the drinks. And we sucked down three of them, and a plate of oversalted but deliciously burned roasted Brussels sprouts, and somewhere in there Willum told me What Being Metrosexual Means to Him. He laid it out in paragraphs like a college entrance essay, and when he got to the full body wax, I spilled my new drink over the rim in embarrassed laughter and blurted that I'd never been with a man who had a waxed anything, and he flushed and murmured, "I'll show you. I'll show you my chest if you want . . ." Jesus.

Well, I guess I wanted. It had been four months, and that had been a visiting colleague at a symposium we'd hosted—an old friend and classmate from Princeton—and I'd been so worried about my reputation, and he'd been so worried about his wife, that neither of us had much fun. I suppose his worry should have canceled out mine, but it didn't. After he was gone, I was left with a metallic taste in my mouth and mild depression and I wondered how Frith the Intrepid, sometime Nordic Queen, had become such a ninny, and I felt worse.

So Willum and I told the waitress to hold our tab, and we leaned together shoulder to shoulder and weaved out to my Volvo, which was way back in the shadows of the hedge on Elm Street. We slid laughing into the back seat, and he unbuttoned his shirt and: Lo and behold, his chest was smooth as a baby's. I slid my open palm over it with the same fascination with which I had touched those weavings, and of course my hand slid down over his taut hairless stomach to his waistband and I found myself mumbling, *What else is that smooth?* And whoa, it was. He had a hard-on, and the launchpad was as smooth as his chest; he must have had a very recent wax job. And that led to pants sliding down and me thanking God I was wearing a skirt. Well, it was fun. Really, really fun. We laughed the whole time and shouted, I think. It was such a surprise. Why didn't we use a condom? We were fools. Total, complete fools. I'd never done it in a car. I liked how the springs or the shocks or whatever got into the swing of it. And I even remembered in flagrante the racy e.e. cummings poem "She Being Brand New," and it didn't ruin anything.

Willum and I had a few more rolls, on legitimate beds, all fun. And then we had the inevitable talk: *This can't go on*—and we were both relieved. And then I missed my period. And then we had the dad talk—the No Dad conversation—and we were both sort of relieved again.

So now I'm a mom-in-waiting—ten weeks, no nausea yet. And whenever I enter the department office he flushes like a radish, right down his neck and onto his trout-smooth collarbones. And he actually bats his eyelids, which slays me. The ginger way we treat each other, the respectful, completely off-the-subject conversations—it's all quite lovely. God, I sound British. Now I really am nauseous.

But sometimes I think, *I'm going to be a mom! A mom! And the dad is kind and sweet and intelligent! And I don't have to have anything to do with him! Yay! This is way better than being married!*

I know that maybe I'm kidding myself. But growing up with Hayley, I don't really have any other template.

*

I got away from my father, the news of his dying. Hayley, Mom, drank the tea I brought her on the porch and hugged me close to her on the bench with her free arm. I knew even then that this was a time not to ask a bunch of questions, so I didn't. But after a while she said, "Did I ever tell you how I met your dad?"

I shook my head.

"I was a postdoc," Hayley said. I didn't ask what that was. "I had just finished the first book of poems, the translations, and I was invited to a translators' conference at Tulane, which is down in Louisiana. In New Orleans. Do you know where that is?"

Of course I did. I was trying to read *Interview with the Vampire,* which was tough going. I told you I was precocious.

"We had a free Saturday, and one of the offerings was an airboat ride in the bayou. The swamp. They have a huge flooded forest in South Louisiana called the Atchafalaya Basin. I love the name. Atchafalaya. I'd read about it. The Cajuns live all around it, even in it, and they still run strings of crawfish traps and still speak a version of French, and the music, Pup—gaw!

You know how great it is. That Cheryl Cormier CD—she's your cousin, by the way.

"So anyway, seven of us signed up, and we got picked up in a van before daylight and drove west up Highway 10, which runs miles and miles on tall pilings over the flooded woods. I could see them in the first light. And then we took an exit at a town called Henderson and bumped down a rough road to a bunch of low buildings and a boat ramp and a long dock over the cove with a honky-tonk at the end of it. That's like a bar. A sign said WHISKEY RIVER. Now I could see a bunch of huge cypress trees standing in the water, some dead.

"There were two airboats, these skiffs with big fans on the back. We were given lifejackets and told to split up, to climb on one or the other. One was captained by a bear of a man with a big beard and a safari hat and a khaki safari vest with a patch that said GATOR RODEO on the back. He did all the talking, kinda loud. He said, 'I'm Gator, that's Johnny.' Johnny, the other captain, was a skinny kid my age, late twenties, in jeans and a Joe Williams Blues T-shirt who hadn't said a word and wouldn't look at any of us. No hat, just a blue bandanna tied around his neck. Whose boat would you have picked?"

"Pop's!"

"Right. But remember, we'd never met. If someone had said right then, 'See that Cajun boy yonder? He's going to be the father of your child!' I would have laughed and bet ten million dollars on the spot, no way.

"Anyway, I picked him. And as I climbed on, he reached out a hand without looking at me and said, 'Careful, cha,' and helped me up. 'Cha' is short for *chère*, which means 'dear.' In the softest voice, with the strongest accent. When he said 'careful,' he didn't pronounce the *r* at all. Caeful. But it was so beautiful. He was skinny, but his hand was rough and strong, I could feel it, and I could feel the strength that ran from his arm, his whole being. Like he was this coiled wild thing beneath this still exterior. Kind of like the swamp itself. I was fascinated, just sorta thunderstruck.

"We took off. Mr. Gator Rodeo zoomed away up the bayou with a great roar. Not Johnny Cormier. He glided the three of us out into the river, gentle as a leaf in the wind. And after a couple of miles, just as the sky was getting all fiery and red with sunrise through the dense trees, he turned up a little blackwater bayou, which is like a still creek, and pushed into a forest with no dry land anywhere. All the trees, the cypress with these big buttress roots and huge overhanging canopies draped with herons and ibis and roseate spoonbills—pink birds like flamingos—and snow-white egrets. And the tupelo trees, more slender, were all perched with woodpeckers and kingfishers, a few big hawks. My jaw must have been hanging open. And all along the little slough were mats of floating water hyacinth, all dappled with lavender flowers, and with nutria, like little beavers, running over them. And alligators! You could see them hiding all along the edges of the channels, usually just the eyes sticking up. Johnny cut the engine and we drifted and then you could hear the basin in its glory. The birdcalls and the slap of a fish jumping, a beaver tail, the almost deafening thrum of the tree frogs and cicadas and locusts. *Roomroomroom.*"

"Wow," I said.

"I know. And Johnny not saying a word, just humming softly. He hummed. Very high, what I would've called a mountain tenor, except that there were no mountains for five hundred miles. And I found myself listening to this quiet hum over all the wild sounds of the swamp. It was very sweet. Some Cajun songs—it had those melodies and cadence. I recognized the tune to 'The Back Door,' 'La Porte d'en Arrière.' Like this, remember?"

She hummed a few bars and I nodded. "Yes, and he didn't even know he was humming, I don't think. He was looking off into the forest, his eyes following the slow, almost luminous flight of a great egret. He seemed somehow so pure standing at the stern of the boat, a little stooped, his hair sticking out a little, his focus, like he was as wholly part of the forest as any of the birds—"

"Pop!" I yelled. I couldn't contain myself.

"Unh-huh," Hayley nodded. She took a sip of the tea, continued. "One of the other girls, a grad student from Iowa who decided to come on a swamp tour in a denim miniskirt—she must have noticed too, because she said too loudly, 'Captain Johnny, can you sing for us? You have a very beautiful voice.' The lovely humming stopped cold. I once saw my father shoot a duck. How it tumbled straight down out of the air. It was like that. He straightened up and gave us all the most startled, apologetic smile, and rubbed his forehead with the back of his arm and started up the big fan and off we went again. I felt like punching her."

"Why didn't you?"

"Because the mosquitoes were already taking care of her." Hayley smiled for the first time that morning.

*

She was in a reverie, remembering, because for what seemed like forever she sipped her tea and looked over our orchard and had this weird smile on her face. I was in thrall to the story. This was a good one. I was hoping that somehow the miniskirt girl fell in and was eaten.

"So? So what happened next?"

"What?" Hayley said. "Oh. Well, we toured for probably three hours. We never saw the other boat. Johnny didn't even have a watch on. But he ran us up into the narrowest paths through the forest, and every once in a while he stopped at a blue ribbon tied to a tree or branch and there'd be a rope angling down into the water and he'd haul it up and there was a crawfish trap at the other end—kind of a metal cage with a wire funnel and a bait bag, like a lobster trap—remember in Maine?" I shook my head. "Right, you were only a few months old. Well, the wire trap would be full of glossy brown crawfish with red bellies, all crawling all over each other. And the obnoxious miniskirt girl would shriek and cover her eyes, she was that freaked out. 'Agh!' she cried. 'They're like bugs! You *eat* those?' Johnny just smiled his bemused smile, didn't say a word. He wasn't humming anymore, she'd taken care of that, but he was moving, rocking still to the music in his head, and his fingers sometimes moved like they were working the strings of a guitar. Anyway, he figured while he was out here he might as well check a few of his traps. It was certainly all the same to us. Except for La Bimba, Miss Miniskirt, we thought it was fascinating.

"When he turned the boat around and began weaving his way back through the forest like he was on any sidewalk, I was sorry. It was the best time I'd had since I could remember. I'd been working really hard on my book, which I also loved, and there was something really simple and pure about this man and about his connection to nature, the water, the birds that I recognized. It was a lot like the poets I was working with, the Tang poets of over a thousand years ago. It's what they were writing about. They all wrote about heartbreak and loss and how hard it is to find true, meaningful things in a dusty world—a world made dusty by human beings—but they found them in nature. It was weird, Pup, like whoa—everything I'd been devoted to in the past bunch of years seemed to be represented in this man. Who was also gentle and kind, I could tell.

"So I really could have stayed out there all day, all month, for the rest of my life."

"Then we would have lived in a swamp!"

"Then we would have lived in Catahoula. And gone shopping in New Iberia."

“Sing that song again! Please, Mom.” She looked at me sideways and half hummed and half sang “La Porte d’en Arrière.” I kicked my legs on the bench, I was so happy.

“Then what?” I insisted.

“Then we got back to the dock and he helped me off, and as I grabbed his strong hand, I felt something zing between us, like electricity.”

“Whoa!”

“I know. And he crinkled down his eyes, which I noticed now were the most beautiful dark green, almost brown but not, and he said again, softly, ‘Careful, cha.’ Then, ‘Not too careful.’ And he looked right into my eyes for the first time and smiled—which was like the sun coming from behind the clouds and lighting up the whole bayou. He said, ‘Maybe you want to come dancing with me later?’

“I was taken aback. I mean, my foot was midstep from the boat to the dock and I was gripping his hand, and I said, ‘*Me?*’ Like, shouldn’t he be asking La Bimba sexpot over there? I stepped onto the planks and I smiled and said, ‘Where?’ ‘Right here,’ and he motioned his head toward the end of the dock, the honky-tonk called Whiskey River. Then he looked away. He really was shy.”

Hayley sipped. “What’d you say? What’d you say?” I cried.

“You know what I said.”

"Say it! Say it!"

"I said, 'That's tonight, right? Well . . .' I didn't know what to do. The van was leaving after lunch and New Orleans was two hours away and there was a whole afternoon and evening till dancing. Your father, Johnny Cormier, was a sensitive soul. I think he must've seen my eyes go to the van parked above the boat ramp, the struggle in my face. 'They leavin', huh?' he said gently. I nodded. 'Tell you what, you come crawfishing with me,' except he said it like 'you come crawfishin' wit me,' in the way that was starting to just kill me. 'If you want. I gotta run the traps. I'll pack us a cooler. And then we can go dancing after. And then I'll drive you back to Tulane." He looked away. I was shocked. That he knew where we were coming from, the university. And that he was offering me this. I said yes, of course. 'I mean, sure. Why not?'

"Why not? Until I had you, Pup, that may have been the happiest afternoon of my life."

I kicked my legs. This was the best. "Then what?"

"Then we got in his johnboat—it's a little low, flat, dark green aluminum boat with an outboard motor. And we ran all through the bayou pulling up the traps, and he showed me how to use the bagging table and put them all in the mesh sacks. He had packed a cooler with ice and Dr Pepper and fish fillet sandwiches and it was the best lunch I ever ate. We ate in the shade of the tupelo on the edge of a little lake, like a clearing way out in the forest, with the egrets flying across and Johnny humming. That night we went dancing, and that wild part I mentioned, that coiled thing inside him?

Well, it unleashed, and he twirled and lifted me around that dance floor until I thought I might faint. From joy, more than anything. Never aggressive, he never threw me around, not once, it was always just the way he had driven that airboat—smooth, Pup, right in sync with the territory, which in this case was the music. And me. Oh, God, I'd never experienced anything like it. We were in that big room lined with tables at the end of that dock, right over the swamp, and it was all open screen, and the band had two guitars and an accordion, a fiddle, a singer named Catherine, and it was packed, and I thought I was in some dream.

"We had two beers all night; the rest of the time we just drank ice-cold soda water and danced. We shut the place down. Catherine said, 'Aw, my dear ones, we got to go out *la porte d'en arrière* now, so we closing with that one.' Pup, there was something about the warmth of it all. Of Johnny, of the band, of the other dancers. I'd never known anything like it. It was real. It was real . . ."

And then Mom began to cry. She went from what seemed so happy in her memory to the most unconstrained grief I'd ever heard. She sobbed. She shook. At first she squeezed me, and I could feel her shaking hard, and then she released me to travel on her own into a territory of loss. It scared me. I think now of the multiple losses of Johnny Cormier. What must have happened to him, to his spirit when he followed her to Denver to her teaching gig at DU. When he traded his johnboat for a food truck, the bayou for the streets of LoDo and West Highland. And then the further distances from his truth, his own truths that he had grown up with and held to in the wandering waterways and woods of the Atchafalaya. How shy he was, how fragile maybe, how the swamp he loved had kept him centered. And his restrained wild energy that Hayley talked of—where that must have gone when he became deeply unhappy in a city in a high desert a universe away from Jeanerette. And then drugs.

She wept, I guess, for all those losses of the man she loved so deeply.

*

Later that morning, we heard the sound of a car coming up the road to the pullout by the pond and thought it was Rosie, arriving unannounced as she always did. To play a marathon round of horseshoes, maybe, or to take us swimming in the quarry she had talked about a few times. It would have been a good day—the morning warmed to something sultry and heavy, almost hot. It was the first of May. Hayley announced it after passing the chicken calendar nailed to the right of the door. May Day. I wasn't sure what was supposed to happen on May Day. Neither was Hayley, except that the first blossoms were beginning to haze the orchard with a dusting of white, like a light snow, and we could smell them coming through the open windows all night. She would have registered the appearance of a recurring motif in the poetry she translated: the fruit tree blossom—cherry or apple or quince—that symbolized purity, rebirth, the ephemeral nature of beauty. The blossoms that never failed to blow down.

The car engine stopped down at the pullout by the pond where Rosie always parked and then it revved again and came on and we stood on the porch and watched a pickup climb our steep track. It was an old truck, not the vintage of Oliver but square-nosed, patched with fiberglass over a body that had originally been green, and it sat up on oversize tires and sounded like it had a cough. It turned in below and parked in the grass between two apple trees. A small man in a black leather jacket climbed down. It was Sci-Fi from the Raiders. The littlest one who had tried to give me regulation horseshoes. I liked him, he'd called me a pro.

"I'll be damned," Hayley murmured. It had already been kind of a momentous morning. Bear was on the porch, barking his head off. His hackles were up. "God!" Hayley cried and tugged his collar and dragged him, claws scrabbling on the porch, and locked him inside, where he continued to raise a ruckus.

Sci-Fi, seeing it was now maybe safe, let go of the door handle and got his boots planted and turned and took in the old orchard and then our mini horseshoe pit and blinked up at us like he was lost.

"I been here," he said. "Before, before."

"Hi!" I called.

He lifted his hand. "I ain't come for that," he said. For what, I had no idea. I looked up at Mom, who shrugged. "I got something," he called.

"Come up!" Hayley said. He didn't. He was such a strange dude. He went to the back of the truck and reached up to the bed and tugged hard and slid out a deer, which slithered onto the ground. No antlers, a doe. Hayley and I just stood there. If an alien had landed in the orchard and emerged carrying a cube of steaming kryptonite, I'm not sure we would have been more at a loss.

"Roadkill," he said. "Good. Just now." Then he bent to the hind legs and began to drag it up the slope. At that we broke from our trance and ran down to meet him and help him half drag, half carry the deer to the porch. She didn't look like roadkill; she had a neat bullet hole right behind her shoulder.

"What's that?" I said, putting my finger on the bloody fur. Sci-Fi looked at me with his two-color eyes and said, "Where the car hit." Hayley and I glanced at each other. He smiled with one side of his mouth. He had a teardrop tattoo descending from his left eye. "You got a freezer?" he said. Hayley shook her head. "Oh." That seemed to stop the proceedings in their tracks. "We have a half fridge. Propane," Hayley said.

Sci-Fi stood and surveyed our domain from the porch, then looked down at his gift. "Benjy said she only got one dress." He nodded at me. "I figured maybe you could use some meat."

Benjy was in my class. My one-day-a-week class at the Putney Elementary School. He was super shy and liked to build things with Legos in the corner whenever we had playtime. I burned with embarrassment. I was mortified. If *he* noticed I came in my Monday Best every Wednesday, well . . .

"Oh, wow," Hayley said. She wasn't sure whether to be grateful or alarmed or what.

"Back in the truck," Sci-Fi said. He blew out. "I got a freezer." We helped him drag the doe back down the hill and he tied a rope to her head and climbed up and in and we lifted and all three of us got her up and over the tailgate. He climbed back in the driver's seat and waved at us and ground the reverse gear and coughed back down the hill.

"Crap," Hayley said. We heard the engine snort and rev as he turned onto the county road. "I guess we've gotta get you a new dress."

*

Sci-Fi came back the next day on his motorcycle, which he parked by the pond. We never saw it, but we heard it. A thunderous herald of conflict and apocalypse. And then the little man in black leather emerged from the flowering apple trees. He carried a paper sack. He barely said a word. He blinked at us with his crazy eyes and his twisted smile and handed off the packet. We looked inside.

"Backstrap," he said. In the sack, partially wrapped in wax paper, were two venison roasts from a poached whitetail, frozen hard. He nodded at us a few times and walked back down the track with his hands in his pockets. A very weird dude. Even I knew that, at seven.

He got halfway to the turn where our visitors disappeared and stopped and came back. You can walk away with your hands in your pockets, but you really can't walk toward someone that way, and I could see now he didn't know what to do with his hands. He bent down and grabbed up a windblown branch, pretty big, and carried it back to us. We watched him; it was a strange pageant. He handed me the stick.

"Thanks," I said.

"Uh, you think Ben could come up and fish in the pond sometime?" he said.

Hayley and I both looked at each other and both, at the same time, blurted, "Sure, of course."

Apple and the tree.

*

Sci-Fi had barely gone when another car came up the road. Rosie. She was wearing a one-piece purple swimsuit and a wrap printed with red hibiscus flowers, blue cork sandals. "You-all ready to go to the quarry?" she called. Which was pretty much rhetorical, there being only one answer.

We turned to fetch swim stuff from the cabin, and she said, "Unh-unh, you don't need anything, I've got it all. Towels, lunch, the works. Unless you're particularly modest."

She knew we weren't. Hayley and I always swam in our birthday suits. And I was a very good swimmer already. If Hayley had one guiding principle in child-rearing, it was to raise a daughter who acted a lot of the time like an otter. We whistled for Bear and all four of us sauntered down the dirt track under snowy clouds of apple blossoms.

*

Tonight's snow has abated but not stopped. If I lift my eyes from the desk, they go to the unhurried falling beyond the glass doors, the slow sift in the yellow light of the half-buried patio lamps. I think of a hatch of tiny mayflies backlit at evening over the pond. The mayflies were nearly transparent and burned in sunlight in a suffusion of sparks. The snowflakes have more substance but seem just as ethereal. Maybe it's the silence and the feeling that this snow will fall until the end of time.

I put both hands around the hot tea mug the way Hayley used to do on the bench.

What kind of mother will I be? That's what I wonder as I think about that afternoon. I will take my daughter to the cabin, to the pond. We'll swim at every time of day. I'll share with her the sight of an evening hatch. Of course I will, but. But what?

Will I feel lonely doing it, in a way that Hayley and I never felt? Will I miss my own mother? Will I feel her absence more, in the company of my daughter? Will I not know what to do then, in a way Hayley never, ever didn't know? Because she didn't seem at a loss, not once. She cried, she was brokenhearted, she was uncertain with sudden gifts—like Rosie, like a package of venison, the offerings of friendship. She struggled some nights with her work, I could see it from above, chin over the bed—but she always knew where she was and what to do; or she seemed that way, to me. And together we were never lonely.

This is the thing about missing one's mother this much. I want to call through the silent snow that seems in some way like a veil and reach her on the other side of it and say, "Hey! Hey, it's me, Frith! Who, when she was with you, could be anyone. A queen. An otter. It's *me*! I'm going to have a daughter. A daughter! As you did. Will she be okay? She's not a love child like yours, not born of a love so deep you only spoke of it once, that morning in May—nope. This one is born of a tussle. Careless. Will it be okay to raise her this way? Without a mission? Without the orchard as the center of the world? Without you writing out poems every night beneath us? Without Bear? In this strange twilight of academia with colleagues who are actors and students who are ghosts? Can I show her anything real? Anything true? Is my love enough? Will I teach her to swim, to make syrup, to throw a horseshoe? Will I love her as I loved you?"

I breathe, press the cup. The snow will not stop. It will fall until it obliterates the dusty earth, Frith. That's its job.

*

Black Clouds

Black clouds flock over Tsu Mountain.
Waves roll white on the river.
A pair of cormorants wings fast downstream
racing the darkness.
Tomorrow morning snow may trace the ridges
and I wonder if we have collected enough firewood.
I am too young to be sick with worry.

My little daughter plays on the floor, heedless.
She tosses her hair.
Look at the waterfalls:
The springs fly off the cliffs like braided ribbons.
They don't care which way they are blown.

That was the next poem. I felt then that the poems were talking to me, right to me, personally. What Hayley must have felt as she sorted through them in the lantern light.

Nine

The quarry was very close. Two miles north up the Westminster West Road was a narrow dirt track we'd passed a score of times and never noticed. There was no green road sign: The turn was after the barn at Putney Theater and before the fields of the llama farm, and it took off into the forest and wound up into the hills to the west.

We were all crammed into Rosie's Subaru, with a cooler and a picnic basket and canvas boat bags stuffed with towels. Solid woods on either side and the road got narrower and rougher, until we were jouncing over exposed rocks and the branches of the younger trees scraped the sides of the car like reaching fingers. It was like driving through an aquarium then, a narrow passage through shifting green deeps where the light sprayed down and fractured at watery angles.

Up ahead through the trees I saw blue sky and sunlight, and we bounced out into a grassy clearing. I shoved open the door and Bear and I ran to the edge. Swimming! And green water! I'd never seen water so green. It had the hardness of a jewel, the transparency of glass. It was children's-book green, that's what I thought. And it was set in a bezel of low granite cliffs. At one end, to our right, the hole elongated and the water shallowed and there was a pocket beach at the end of it, of white sand. From the beach, blocks of stone climbed a fissure in the cliff and formed natural steps.

I loved the place at first sight and love it still. I go there in the warm months and know now that the cliffs are only twelve feet off the water. But then they seemed high, daredevil high. I heard cries of *Frith! Careful, Pup!* behind me and turned and saw them unloading the bags and baskets and I shucked my clothes fast and jumped.

I was naked and barefoot, arms held up like wings, and I might have said, "Vroom! Vroom!"—I probably did—and then I cried "Tyr!"—that's the Viking god of war—and I ran straight for the edge and sailed off. How long does it take a seven-year-old Nordic queen to reach terminal velocity? Probably more than twelve feet. But I did not feel that I was plunging. Time, who is so often not our friend, expanded and buoyed my flight. I sailed. I glided. However much of a second I arced in air seemed like a good chunk of my new life as an aviator. I remember blue sky, black granite, green water, and a cordite smell of speed.

And then I hit and I was transmigrated into something submarine, something at one with density, and cold, something with slow fins like a sea turtle whose world was bubbles, and then I was swimming instinctively for the light, and I breached like an albino sperm whale.

I knew all about Moby Dick—Hayley had synopsized the story for me—and I gasped and blinked up into sunlight, which was obliterated by the shadow of my faithful dog, who nearly landed on top of me. Blind loyalty. Twelve feet isn't Acapulco, but it's pretty far for a Bernese mountain mutt. Big splash. Swimming was not his forte, but he loved it, and now he swam at me and clawed me with his nails, trying to save me, I guess, and before I could yell him off, two more projectiles exploded in the green water, my mother and Rosie, both fully clothed. They did not breach like whales but came thrashing into air, and as soon as they snorted and got their bearings, they began to yell at me.

"Let's swim to the beach!" I cried and started off. I am, was, a natural swimmer, and I might not have had a competition freestyle, but I could crawl or sidestroke myself through any amount of well-intentioned turbidity. I think everyone got the message: I was fine. Bear dog-paddled after me, huffing through his nose, and the gals followed.

I've since used the tactic many times: When besieged by chaos, pretend it's not there and swim calmly to the beach. Another lesson: Swimming calms the heart. By the time we all got to the sand, Hayley tackled me, half linebacker, half relieved mom, and said, "Frith Terrel Cormier, what the fuck were you *thinking*?"

I was not afraid of falling. I wasn't, once. It's good to remember that on the verge of motherhood.

Rosie brought her famous potato salad and a roast chicken and cold grilled bratwurst, which is now maybe my favorite thing on earth to eat. And a thermos of iced sweet tea watered down with pink lemonade. She brought red plastic cups in honor of the Raiders.

I was starving. That was another thing I learned that morning: Being brave makes one hungry. We spread a blanket on the beaten grass by the turnaround, more to keep off the ticks than the dirt, and we chowed down. After we let ourselves digest for about ten minutes, we went back to the cliff edge and jumped off it in every combination we could dream up. Hayley jumped with me on her back. Rosie and Hayley and I all jumped off in a line, holding hands. Rosie executed a perfect swan dive. Bear had learned his lesson and planted his forepaws at the lip and barked and barked. Then we went back to the blanket for hot tea, because by then the icy water had chilled us. Rosie went to her Forester and brought out an orange Zihuatanejo beach bag from which she pulled something woolly and handed it to me. It was a tightly knit hoodie sweatshirt in mohair, night blue with maroon bands on the sleeves.

"Here, Wonder Girl," she said. "Put this on."

God, it was soft. And the color was like the sky way up in the dark center of everything when night gathers just after the first stars. "Really?" I said.

"Yes, really," she said. "I made it for you."

*

So: Respite. Joy. Swimming. A hoodie.

The other day, I read a newspaper story about a man confined to a wheelchair his whole life by cerebral palsy who finally realized his dream of going to the beach. There was a picture of him in a lifeguard cap with sand and waves and gulls behind him, his smile as wide, it seemed, as the horizon. He was a black man, maybe in his fifties. My first thought was: Why did it take him so long? And then the self-correction: You, Frith Terrel Cormier, have not a single clue what this man has been through. And then the reflection: This beach was unremarkable. The sand was maybe dirty. The water behind the man was not aquamarine or even really blue. He was not holding a Corona. And he seemed to be so happy. How many beaches have you been to, Frith? Beaches like beads on a bracelet. Where is your gratitude? Why do you feel like you are moving through your life in a haze that smells a little like burning plastic?

Not what I want to communicate to my new daughter, Isabel.

That day I was like the man in the picture, we all were. We were at the Backer Quarry, having a brilliant afternoon. An afternoon always accompanied in memory by the plunge of a shrieking body hitting clear cold water, by a spray of water-dazzling sunlight.

Back on the blanket I was stretched out on my stomach, cheek to the sunbaked wool. I'd stopped shivering. Rosie placed her cool palm on my back and said, "Take a swim nap, why don't you?"

"What's that?"

"Where you've been swimming forever and you're lying on a sun-warmed dock, or blanket, or rock, and you pass out for a while and it's the best thing ever."

"Huh." Didn't sound that fun to me. But I felt the sun on my cheek like a hand and closed my eyes and the insides of my lids were red and floaty with squiggly lines and I must have conked out. When I woke up, I heard Hayley and Rosie laughing and then Rosie whistle out a long sigh and say, "Do you want to hear the story of the Grafton sisters, who were supposed to marry the Ferris brothers? And what happened right here?"

"Are you kidding?" Hayley said.

I was about to sit straight up and yell, "Doh!" when Rosie said, "I better keep it down. It's kind of an adult story."

"Got it."

I opened my eyes the barest crack and saw Rosie adjust the brim of her floppy linen hat and say, "Well . . .

". . . there were two Grafton sisters and two Ferris brothers. The Grafton sisters were descendants of the family that founded Grafton, on the other side of Westminster. They owned a ton of land and had moved into local banking. The

Ferris family were logging and lumber people who saw the coming demise of their industry in this part of Vermont—there were gigantic companies in Maine and in the South who were crushing them—and the Ferrises decided to move into car dealerships." I knew what a car dealership was: Hayley and I had been to one in Keene that smelled like popcorn and Ajax. "Well, car dealerships need banks, and banks just love car dealerships. So what better way to cement the auspicious business dealings of two fine families . . ."

I loved it when Rosie talked like this. I didn't really understand it, but I knew she was acting now. She could get into the head of anyone and talk just like them.

". . . than to marry the brothers to the sisters, younger to younger, older to older. I mean, after all, they all grew up together, were in the same classes in school, liked to play the same sports, were all reasonably attractive—except for maybe the Ferris brothers—and had even been on a date or two."

Rosie adjusted her oversize sunglasses. I adored this. I made myself keep my legs from kicking. "Did they get married?" Hayley urged. "In a double wedding in a cathedral?"

"What do you think?"

"Yes! Because this is a tragedy. And they had reasonably attractive children!"

"Well, let's see." Rosie smiled.

"Yes or no!"

"Let's not get our undies in a bundle."

"Okay, okay." I understood then that Hayley was a lot like me. The way she got in the grips of a story.

"So," Rosie resumed. "The Ferris boys, as I said, weren't really attractive at all. In fact their faces looked a little like baked potatoes. With beady squirrel eyes. And mouths with almost no lips, like a ferret."

"Gross."

"And big ears, kind of like those white fungi you see on trees. Know what I mean?"

"Yes! Yuck!"

"And to tell you the truth, they weren't that smart. They were actually kind of dumb. They were a year apart in age, but they'd been put back a few times and jumbled around and they both ended up in the same class, where they were the biggest students, of course, which they took advantage of by being occasional bullies. Not that occasional."

Rosie lifted the hem of her wrap and patted beads of sweat off her cheeks and the end of her nose. Her cheek was pink and sidelit in the sun and I could see the tiniest colorless hairs fuzzing over it. I had this horrible image of potato-head giants with fungus ears and no lips sitting on poor littler kids and stuffing grass in their mouths.

"But," Rosie said, in her low Let's Let Frith Nap voice, "they were rich. Very rich for these parts, and when they were sixteen, they got a teal Cadillac convertible, '66, with fins and a white top, cherry. Shiny and perfect. They got it to share. And they were very good athletes, despite not being able to remember the plays, so they were always in the paper, running over poor kids from Springfield and Montpelier and Keene and scoring touchdowns."

The world of school athletics was brand-new to me this year, and from my glancing acquaintance with football games under the lights and cheerleaders and jocky kids, and girl soccer players who thought they were better than everyone else, I'd already decided that it was pretty much the dumbest thing ever. Hayley and I had tried one high school football game in Brattleboro and we'd lasted ten minutes.

"So anyway, the Grafton sisters had grown up with the Ferris family and had been to every Ferris picnic and Fourth of July party and Christmas bash, and they'd been generally brainwashed to believe that these two brothers would one day be their husbands. Now, these girls, Marjorie and Beth, short for Bethesda, *were* attractive. Beth, the older by a year, had hair the color of honey and dark blue eyes, kind of smoky, like this blanket."

"Whoa."

"Right? And she was supersmart and played the violin like an angel. Oh, and was a nationally ranked tennis player, and starred in the school production of *The Sound of Music*. Stop! You're moving your feet just like Frith."

"Sorry, sorry. What about Margie?"

"Marjorie. She was the sweet one. She was kind to everyone, and she had a special shed in the backyard, where she rehabilitated hurt hawks and baby crows that fell out of their nests. And her hair was auburn—like yours."

"Ha!"

"And the two sisters were a year apart in school and they were best friends, of course. Hey, there goes a Cooper's hawk. See? The dark tail bands and the orange breast?"

I almost sat up. I had seen it glide over earlier, sliding down a current of air into the tops of the trees across the quarry. But right now my attention was on the Grafton girls.

"Then what?" Hayley said. "The girls were in high school, right?"

"Yes. Beth was a senior, about to graduate. She had gotten a scholarship to Pomona, way out in California, where she was going to study genetics. And Marjorie was an even better student, and had already been contacted by the biology department at Stanford. One other thing: The girls were famous for their pies, and they made fruit leather that they sold at school."

Rosie sat up off her folded legs and stretched her long arms and sat back on the blanket cross-legged. I shifted my head just a little but kept my eyes mostly closed. She had big feet, with bony bumps under the big toes she told me were called bunions, from when she took ballet lessons.

"Just about this time, there was a big party in Brattleboro at the Eatons' house, the real estate brokers. And there was *beer* and loud music and Beth's and Marjorie's friend Elly got drunk and disoriented and went upstairs to one of the bedrooms to lie down. And the Ferris brothers noticed her and followed, and they went in and locked the door and did bad things."

It was like the air pressure dropped. I couldn't breathe. I wasn't really sure what bad things boys did to disoriented girls, but it clenched my chest. I couldn't see Hayley's face, but I knew exactly how troubled it would look. But she didn't interrupt. Rosie nodded slightly to acknowledge the concern and continued.

"Elly didn't tell a soul, but she didn't go to school the next day or the next, and the rumor was she got alcohol poisoning. But after a few days Beth and Marjorie, who were a couple of her closest friends, went by her house to see her. And Elly broke down and told them everything."

I couldn't keep my eyes off Rosie's face. I didn't know what to do with my legs.

"Then what?" Hayley murmured.

"About the same time, the sisters' parents had prodded them to go on a double date with guess who? The brothers called and asked and the sisters flat-out refused. Which the brothers, being the brothers, couldn't fathom. They waited a few days and called again. Again the girls were busy. And then Elly, who still hadn't shown up back at school, was put on suicide watch, because her parents were afraid she might harm herself."

"God," Hayley whispered.

Rosie exhaled. "Well. About a week after that, the Ferris brothers got kind of pushy and cornered the sisters after fourth period and said they had big Saturday-night plans with the Caddy—that's the fancy convertible—and the girls would be crazy not to join them. Beth and Marjorie looked at each other, just for a split second, like a coded language, and then they nodded and said, 'Yeah, okay, sure. It'll be fun. See you then.' "

Rosie looked toward the pond. "A light breeze has come up. Look how the water shimmers. I adore that shade of green."

"Me too," Hayley said softly. "What happened next?"

Rosie straightened her back and stretched one bent arm into the sunlight. "Wanna let Frith nap and go for another swim?" she said.

"You said something happened here!" Hayley cried. "What happened?"

"Oh, that. Well, the next Saturday the brothers picked the girls up in the Cadillac. The boys were almost charming, giddy even. They held the doors open for the sisters, gave them corsages like it was prom. They said they'd go to the Polka Dot Diner for an early dinner of burgers and malts, and then maybe they'd go watch the sunset up at the Backer Quarry. Right here. Well, the girls exchanged a look because they knew what that meant."

"What did it mean? Parking, right?"

"Right. Making out with Potato Face One and Two."

The grotesque image again, having to kiss the no-lips of the potato-head brothers. Hayley groaned. "Ahhhh!"

"That's just what I'm sure Beth and Marjorie were thinking. Because, you see, they'd had a whole week to ponder their situation. All the pressure from their families. These rich bullies.

"So they all went out to the diner and had burgers and malts, and then just as it was getting dusky, they drove up to the quarry. To right here. And parked." She pointed to a gravelly patch right at the edge of the steepest part of the cliff. I could see it if I lifted my head an inch. "And the girls grinned and Beth said, 'Hey, boys, look what we brought,' and they produced two silver flasks full of whiskey. 'Let's warm things up!' they said. Well, the boys thought this was their lucky day, their luckiest day ever. They knew from experience that there was nothing more fun than a drunk girl, especially a good girl who never drank."

"Yuck."

"So the girls passed around the flasks, and when it came to their turns, they tipped them back and pretended to drink. And when the boys tried to lean over and kiss them—one couple in the front seat, one in back—they pawed them and ripped their tops. But the girls fended them off and put their fingers to their lips and said, 'You just be patient! You'll get *everything* you want in just a few minutes.' The boys were beside themselves. They thought they'd gone to heaven. And they got drunk. Drunker. And then Beth said, 'Now we're going to surprise you with something really naughty.' And the boys' eyes got big. 'But first let's play this game that you're our love prisoners and we're transporting you to love jail.' "

Maybe my eyes were wide open, I don't know. I'd never heard such a story.

" 'Where we will make you do bad things,' the girls said. The boys thought that was the best idea ever. Being bad was their thing. They were about out of their minds. And the sisters produced two hanks of braided apricot leather from their purses.

"And apricot leather is really tough, the homemade kind, which you know if you've ever bitten off a hunk." Hayley nodded. "Well, the girls had made these two ropes out of apricot leather, which they braided tightly. It was really strong. Beth smiled all lovey at Ryan, the oldest, and said, 'It's just apricot leather. Here, bite off a chunk.' He did and grinned. Yum. 'We can *eat* it later,' she said, which drove him more wild. So she had him put out his wrists, and she tied him tightly to the steering wheel. Then Marjorie produced her own apricot leather rope and had the younger Artie lick it."

"Oh, gross!" Hayley cried.

"Yep, gross. And then she had him put his wrists together and tied him tightly to the door handle, the one you grab. 'You are bad, bad boys,' they said, 'and we are taking you to *love jail.*' The boys laughed like hyenas. And then the girls slipped off the seats and out the doors and blew the brothers kisses and said, 'Just wait one minute.' But before they slammed the doors, Beth released the emergency brake and chopped the shifter down into neutral so the car could roll. And then they ran to the back and put their shoulders between those fins and shoved. You can see it's a little downhill to the edge. It didn't take much of a push."

Rosie said, "Your mouth is open."

"Did the car roll over the *edge*?"

"Yep. Rolled off and sailed through the air—there was less water then, so the drop was higher—and hit and slowly sank. The girls ran to the edge to watch."

I felt queasy. Hayley looked over at the scene of the crime. "Is that true?" she said.

"Yes, it is. The girls walked slowly back to the Westminster West Road and sat on a rock just up the track for a couple of hours and swatted the occasional mosquito and watched the lightning bugs. At about midnight they took deep breaths and stood, tidied their torn dresses as best they could, and started walking down the pavement."

"Why did they sit in the dark?" Hayley said.

"Because they wanted to wait for the apricot-leather ropes to dissolve. They had done the experiment in a bucket, and they knew that in ice-cold water it took about three hours for the leather to liquefy. So they gave it four."

"Oh, wow." Hayley was sitting straight up on the blanket, leaning forward a little, like anyone listening to a ghost story. Which, in a way, is what this was. "They'd also tied each other up with it, by the wrists, to experiment, and they knew it was pliable enough. It was sort of gummy and soft. Soft enough not to leave rope burns when you struggled against it for a minute or two."

This was really scary. I couldn't help but think of the awful brothers down under the dark water, tied to their Cadillac with pieces of fruit and struggling while they drowned. They were really bad and all, but still.

"God," Hayley murmured.

Rosie blew out, propped herself up with straight arms to stretch her back. "Yes," she said. "It's famous in these parts."

"So what happened next?"

"Well, the two sisters walked down the road. It was late, as I said, and so they didn't really expect to get picked up. They figured they'd have to walk to the llama farm, which back then was Silas Caldwell's dairy farm. But it was Friday night, and there'd been a party at the Dines' house, a bunch of college kids who'd just come back from school.

"So the girls see a wash of headlights in the trees, and who comes around the corner but Carrie Peacock and Dorian Yates and Melissa Gillis and Gina Giobbi all stuffed into an ancient station wagon with *four* boys crammed into the back. Carlton and your neighbor Geordie and William and Arnold, big boys, all locals from around West Hill, and all laughing up a storm, everyone three sheets to the wind except Carrie, who was driving. The sisters heard the car coming before they saw it and had time to smudge some dirt on their faces and hyperventilate—I've never seen you look so horrified."

"I truly am," Mom said.

"I get it. Do you want me to go on?"

"Is a trout watertight?"

"Right. Okay. So they hyperventilated and got in a couple of practice sobs. And when the headlights caught them, they were crying and their dresses were ripped and they were dirty. They were a mess. And that almost got them. Almost sent them to the slammer."

"It did?"

"Yep, I'll explain in a minute." Rosie smiled. She had a beautiful smile. She wasn't a witch, she was our Rosie. I was just learning that she had a dark side, and that maybe all artists, even Li Xue, had it too.

"The car came around the bend and lit up the sisters and Carrie slammed on the brakes. Everybody piled out. Carrie, the only one sober—except for the sisters—held up her hands and made everybody quiet down and she said, 'What on *earth* happened to you girls?' The girls' faces crumpled and they wept. They really wept now. I mean full-on sobbed.

"Maybe it was dawning on them what they'd done. I mean, before it was all about vengeance and justice for their friend, and about getting out of a terrible trap with two really horrible young men. But now that other people had shown up, and shined a light, so to speak, on them and their deed . . . well. This gave them a sudden moment of self-reflection and caused them to finally fall apart. They'd done a horrendous thing. Taking a life, any life, even a trout's, is serious business, as you know."

"Right," Hayley said. "Right," I whispered to myself. I felt grown up just then. I think I sensed that this story was some sort of rite of passage. Maybe Rosie was giving us, as a kind of gift, a moral tale that she knew I would chew over for the rest of my life. And that it would influence me, somehow. Because I have wondered to this day if she knew I was listening all along. Something about the way she pitched the story, avoided certain images, explained stuff just a little. I have asked her since and she denied it. I'm not sure.

"The sisters cried and cried," Rosie continued. "They were comforted by the older girls from the car, and the boys stood around in a protective circle, wanting to help and not knowing quite what to do. And little by little, the sisters got out the story. How the boys took them on a car date and they were having pretty much fun, but then the boys got drunk and attacked them, and they fought them off in the car, and in the struggle Ryan must have knocked the shifter and the car started to roll and Beth screamed and they both freed themselves from the clutches of the brothers and jumped out. Barely got out before the car rolled over the edge. And they heard the splash. And they leaned over the edge and saw the car sinking, the car lights in the water, which doused after a few seconds, and they called and called in the pitch-dark. But the boys were drunk, as they said, and they must have swallowed water or hit their heads on impact. The sisters shouted and shouted and finally ran down the road for help.

“The group of older kids just listened with their mouths open, like you are now.” She poked Hayley in the ribs. The sun had slid over a degree or two, and Rosie turned a little and pulled down one side of the hat brim. She looked to me like a movie star.

“When Beth and Marjorie got to the end of the tale, Carrie went straight to the back of the station wagon and pulled out two frayed Mexican blankets that the boys had been sitting on and wrapped them around the sisters. Then she began issuing orders. Carrie always knew the right thing to do. She said that she and the girls would drive the sisters straight to Putney, which was only ten minutes away, and they would wake someone up and call the police. Then they would drive to the hospital in Brat, straight to the ER, to get the girls some help. They were obviously in shock. The four boys would run up the dirt road to the quarry and see if there was any chance of rescuing the brothers. And that’s what they did.

"Within ten minutes over a dozen squad cars, ambulances, fire trucks were speeding to the quarry, not to mention volunteer firefighters and search-and-rescue folks. Half the county's phones were ringing. Which the sisters realized was a boon, because even in their traumatized state they knew that this wasn't being treated as a crime but as a rescue operation, and that all the traffic and the well-meaning first responders would trample all over everything and completely contaminate the crime scene. It would be very hard to prove anything critical, like exactly where the car was parked and just how close to the edge it had been.

"The sisters were no dummies, remember. They had rehearsed and rehearsed their story, and that's what they told the two detectives who came to the hospital the next morning. But . . ."

She stopped. "But what?" Hayley cried.

"The detectives were a man and a woman. Karla Creigh and Nils Mathiesson. Both extremely sharp, both veterans of city police departments who had moved to southern Vermont for bucolic peace and serenity. Ha!"

Bucolic sounded like *broccoli*.

"The girls were at Brattleboro General, in bed, resting. Kept until late morning just as a precaution. They had scratches, Beth had a bruise on her arm, and they had been in shock, so. Anyway, the detectives listened to each one separately, scribbled in their little notebooks, nodded, glanced at each other.

Both stories matched exactly, surprise surprise. But something puzzled them. It was that the boys had both been found lying *inside* the convertible. Artie was draped over the door—remember, the top was down—and Ryan had settled down on the front seat . . ."

I noticed through cracked lids that Hayley was watching me now, a little worried, wondering if, after all, I had heard the whole story. I made my eyes close; I made a soft snoring sound. Too late now. She let Rosie go on.

"And the detectives knew that the events as described would most likely have sent the boys out of the car on impact. They didn't have any problem believing that two very drunk teens might have drowned after that fall and that impact—even athletes like the brothers—but what bothered them was the position of the bodies. How—why—had they stayed in the car? It was surely possible, but not likely.

"And then Officer Creigh leaned toward Marjorie in her bed and said, 'Why were your faces smudged with dirt?'

" 'What?' Marjorie stammered. The question had caught her completely off guard.

" 'The girls who picked you up said you really looked like wrecks, that your faces were smirched with dirt. It was confirmed by the ER nurses who cleaned you up. But you said you all had driven straight from the diner and had parked in the car and that's when the boys tried to assault you.' Officer Creigh kept her voice gentle and her face straight.

"Marjorie gawped. She swallowed. She started to say something, and then Beth piped up. The curtain between their beds had been drawn closed, but she had overheard the question. 'Pull the curtain!' she called. It startled everyone. They did.

"'We did it,' she said. Now Marjorie's eyes got huge, staring at her sister. 'We did it by the Westminster West Road before we started walking toward the llama farm. We smudged our faces with dirt.'

"Marjorie gaped. She couldn't believe it. Officer Creigh cocked her head. This was interesting. 'Why?' she said gently.

"'Because,' asserted Beth, 'we wanted everyone to believe us about the attacks, the attempted whatever. So you wouldn't—so everyone wouldn't—blame us for jumping out of the car and not going over the edge with the boys.'

"Silence. It had the ring of truth. It *was* true, in its way. And it was tinged with embarrassment and shame.

"'Did you rip your dresses?' Creigh asked. 'Did you scratch yourselves?'

'No, we didn't,' Beth said firmly. 'The brothers did that all on their own.'

"That also had the ring of truth. Nothing ever in the world sounded truer. Creigh and Mathiesson had been doing this a long time, and they knew she wasn't lying. And the autopsies bore it out, as they found traces of skin and blood under the brothers' fingernails."

Rosie stretched, took off her sunhat, rubbed her forehead, replaced the hat. "I think we should go for one more swim, don't you?"

"Wait! Wait! What happened after that? I mean with the girls and everything?"

"Well, the detectives always had their suspicions. Ever afterward. I'm very good friends with Rob Hallowell, who was one of the assistant DAs at the time. But there was no way they could bring a case against the girls. Everyone from Boston to Burlington believed their story, why wouldn't they? And there was absolutely no other corroborating evidence. So case closed, poor, poor traumatized girls. And Beth went off to Pomona and became a doctor, a very good one, a pulmonologist, and Marjorie, who seemed to be steeled and toughened by the whole experience, became a fierce environmental lawyer. The end."

"What happened to Elly?"

"Remarkably, she came back to school. She got a degree in psychology, and she runs an animal rescue shelter in Burlington."

The story ended, but the ring of it, its import, kept sounding and sounding like the tones of a deep bell. Finally, Hayley coughed into her fist. She said, "And how do *you* know the true story?"

Rosie swiveled her head and looked at Hayley. "Because Beth was my best friend. Since we were in diapers. Before she died, she told me everything. She said she couldn't hold on to it anymore. She died of pancreatic cancer four years ago. She was convinced that keeping the secret all those years had made her sick."

Mom stared at Rosie. She cleared her throat. "Did she regret the act?"

"She said that had she known she would grow up to kill a man, even a man trying to assault her, she would have chosen not to be born."

Ten

Hayley got invited to a poetry translators' conference in Wyoming. Many famous poets were attending, including her favorite Tang dynasty translator, W. S. Merwin. She had accepted the invitation the previous fall and forgotten about it, in typical Hayley fashion.

Hayley was so immersed in her own translations and the daily conduct of our lives that distant future plans tended to get rain-washed and overgrown until the vigor of her present circumstances overwhelmed them. In Denver, she'd had help: The comparative literature department's version of Willum was a grousy sixty-year-old named Zelda ("I was destined to go into literature," she always said when she was introduced), and she kept Hayley on track. But out here at the orchard there was no Willum and no Zelda, and I remember Hayley cursing her own abstractedness more than once as she got the prodding letters that likely read, "You haven't responded to our invitation and we still so dearly hope you can attend.

Please let us know at your earliest convenience . . ." Or the more scolding "As you haven't responded to our repeated invitations, we have been forced to cede your place at the Symposium . . ."

Cede your place. The language of self-importance. As if gladiators were vying for the spot. Maybe they were. In any event, we missed stuff because Hayley forgot or procrastinated. But this one she wouldn't miss, because the other poets invited were her gods. These writers she loved almost as much as she loved Li Xue. They were the ones who had inspired her.

So she marked it on the chicken calendar on the wall in bold blue Sharpie, and she made herself check it every week.

After swimming at the quarry and hearing the story of the double murder, I needed a break. That's what I told Hayley. She was outside watering the tomatoes, which were new and tiny, and the spinach and lettuce, which were already leafed out and which we were eating every night. I came up to her where she was singing to herself and I tugged on the hose. She let go of the trigger and the nozzle stopped spraying and dribbled on her bare feet. She tossed it to the ground.

"Yes, Pup?"

"I need a break."

She had her hands on her hips and she took one off and scratched the top of my head.

"You do?"

"Yep. It's a little bucolic around here."

Her eyes flashed and her hand stopped midrub. "Holy shit," she said.

She squatted down and put both hands on my shoulders and her nose was two inches from mine. I could feel her breath on my lips and see the flecks in her green eyes. She said, "You heard the story. The one Rosie told at the quarry."

I nodded.

"Wow." She let her arms come around my back and she pulled me to her tight. She smelled like dirt and grass. I loved that smell. "Did the story get to you?" she said.

I nodded.

"Me too." She let go and studied me. "What do you think of it?" she said. "I mean, what do you think the sisters should have done?"

I shrugged. I didn't know. I still don't. I think that's why the story is so haunting. Was it about forgiveness? Should the sisters have forgiven the brothers for nearly destroying their good friend? Or was the gift Rosie was trying to give me, the rite of passage, an acknowledgment that real evil does exist in the world? And that one of our greatest challenges as humans is to figure out how to resist it, even obliterate it?

I have thought about it, on and off, in all the years since. I think maybe she was trying to tell me that the most powerful attribute of evil is that it invites us to battle it, and in so doing—in the grips of our emotion and in the methods we use—evil propagates itself. It's like one of those superhero villains that grows stronger with every bullet and missile it absorbs.

I wasn't articulating these thoughts then, of course, but I have since. And so Rosie's gift, if that's what it was, was effective.

"I'm thirsty, aren't you?" Hayley said. I nodded. She stood and took my hand and we walked up to the cabin, where she turned off the spigot. She wiped her hands on her overalls, so I did too, and we stepped into the cool of the log house, which even in the middle of the day was always a little dim. From the half-size fridge Hayley pulled a pitcher of squeezed lemonade sweetened with maple syrup, our favorite drink. From the miniature ice tray she salvaged ten tiny pieces of ice and poured two sweating glasses that she adorned with sprigs of mint. We went outside to sit on the porch.

The apple blossoms were falling, detaching themselves with barely a breeze, falling straight into the long grass. Bees were droning among the branches. A professional orchard operation would have mowed all the grass between the rows of trees, but we couldn't manage it. Which was why brambles and spruce and birch saplings were overtaking the edges, even sending outriders into the middle of the orchard.

It was bright out there. We squinted. Hayley had bought us both five-dollar sunglasses from the rack at Rod's Service Station in Putney, and we kept them at the ready on the bench. We both put them on. I thought we looked like celebrities.

Hayley placed the sweating glass against her ruddy cheek and half closed her eyes. So I did too. She moved it down to the side of her neck and I did too, and I felt the pulse in my throat against the glass. She was smiling a little, and I could see from the side that her eyes were fully closed, as if her thoughts had quieted with the touch of the glass, and that she was enjoying the respite.

Mom is very pretty. That's what I thought. A strand of loose, curly hair lay against her temple and the side of the glass, and her tan cheeks were sprayed with freckles.

"Nice, huh?" she said. "And delicious too."

"Yep, delicious," I said.

"You know," she said, not moving the glass. "Good people do bad things."

I knew that.

"My father, your grandfather, was a famous doctor. A psychiatrist. Do you know what that is?"

I nodded. "Like if you're crazy," I said.

"Right. And it turns out there's like a million ways to be crazy, or maybe even just miserable, because of the ways our particular brains tick."

"Got it." We sipped the lemonade and I felt just then, on the bench, part of a privileged circle of noncrazy people, which was nice.

"I told you how I grew up in Canada until I was seven, and how my father ran this sort of hospital where he realized that people with disturbed minds did much better when they were on a farm, where they could participate in meaningful work with others. Like planting and tending a garden or training horses. He was one of the first to write about that."

"Cool. Did they wear orange suits?"

"No!" She tousled my head. "It wasn't a prison."

"Oh."

"Anyway, Mom, your grandmother, was one of the young nurses. She was from Montana, and she idolized your grandfather, who was already almost an old man, and they fell in love and got married."

"And had you!"

"Right. Then he died because he was very old, and Tinny, your grandmother, took me to New Hampshire, where another young nurse from the mental hospital had gotten a job at Dartmouth's Mary Hitchcock Hospital, and got her one there too. And so I was raised in a little town called Enfield. Mascoma, actually, right on a cold-water lake."

"Did you fish and swim?"

"All the time."

"Did you jump off rocks?"

"Of course."

I thought about that. I wondered why we didn't go there; it sounded cool. "How come we don't go visit?"

Hayley drank her lemonade and watched the billowing clouds marching south to north. Today they were high and bright and looked like a parade of puffy animals, most of which had yet to be discovered by science.

"Because," she said, "it makes me sad."

"Because Grandma got killed in a lab?"

"Sort of. She sort of got killed in a lab."

"She got a fever. Because the doctor did something wrong."

"Right. There was a screw-up. The doctor was so brilliant and famous, and he was so on the verge of finding a treatment for this awful deadly fever, he couldn't be bothered to take the very tedious precautions to keep his staff safe from his samples, from the fever. He was sloppy. He was moving too fast."

"The doctor killed Grandma."

"Sort of. I guess he did."

"Did you call the police?"

"Well, it doesn't quite work that way. There was an investigation by a medical panel, and the doctor was censured."

"What's that?"

"Like scolded. But he was allowed to keep his medical license and even continue his important work in the lab, with oversight. In other words, other expert doctors watched what he did closely from then on."

"Oh."

"I know."

"They should have put him in an orange suit. On a chain gang."

She turned and lifted her glasses and studied me. "What have you been reading?"

I shrugged.

"Yep, and he found an effective treatment for this terrible fever and probably saved tens of thousands of lives."

"Oh."

Hayley set the dripping glass on the bench and wriggled her fingers under my hair and placed her hand on the back of my neck. It was cold and wet and felt great.

"That's nice, huh?"

"Wooh. You can keep it there all day."

"It'll get hot in a minute."

"Dang."

"Everybody does bad things once in a while. Sometimes the bad thing is really bad, like with those brothers. Sometimes it's just not doing a good thing, or the right thing."

"Have you done that?"

"Of course. I'm a human being."

"No, you're not." I was only half kidding. Hayley lifted her hand off my neck and pinched the end of my nose before picking up her glass again.

"What did you do? I mean, not do?"

"I hit a deer once with my car. A little deer, probably a yearling. At night, coming back from a party. And she tumbled to the side of the road and got up pretty wobbly and went into the woods. I didn't follow her. Sometimes I think about her in the middle of the night."

"Why?"

"Because the brave and right thing to do would have been to take out the flashlight I had in the glove box and go into the woods to see if she was all right. And if she wasn't, the brave and right thing to do would've been to help her go."

"You mean kill her?"

She nodded. I thought how grown-ups must spend half their time trying to figure out the difference between the right thing and the wrong thing. It seemed pretty tough.

"Li Xue wrote a poem about something similar."

"She did?"

"Wanna hear it?" Mom memorized all her poems. Or she didn't memorize them: In the act of being translated they became threaded into her being, like the animals in Rosie's weavings became a part of the fabric.

"You bet," I said.

She took a long sip and put the glass down and closed her eyes. I closed my eyes too. For a minute we heard only the chirp of a couple of crickets, the tuneless call-and-response of two crows.

She said: "It's called 'Grandmother.' "

Grandmother

The last time I saw you
I let you serve me tea.
You were nearly blind
and as frail as a November leaf
and you shook when you laughed.
You asked what phase the moon was in.
I said, "She's waning, Nainai.
Three more days until the dark of the moon."
You became so still.
In the morning I walked home over the mountain.
Three days later I had word that you were gone.
Now I wish I had told you:
"The moon is waxing, Grandmother.
Tomorrow she will be bright and full!"

I listened to the crows calling, getting fainter and fainter as they flew over the ridge. Hayley had lowered the cold glass, but her eyes were still closed.

I tried to whistle, but it just sounded like air. "It's okay, Mom," I said. "It's just a poem." I put my hand in her lap. She squeezed it and smiled at me. "Was it wrong," I said, "to tell her the truth about the moon?"

"I don't know," she said. "I honestly don't."

"Me neither," I said.

*

Do I know now? I wonder that as I sit at the desk and find the very poem three more sheets down. Truth may be beauty, but it is also heartbreak. That is certain. Because the truest thing, or at least the most certain, is that we will eventually lose everything.

The phone on the desk vibrates. I want to let it buzz, but I am incapable. I pick it up, turn it over. The ID says "Willum." It's 10:07 p.m., a bit late to call anyone. He's been calling. Every few days, just to see how I am faring, which is sweet, but the other evening he called and said, "That was really fun. You know, the other night."

And I thought, the other night was like a month ago. He said, "I was thinking maybe we could do it again. You know, just for fun. No strings attached." So why is it that I was feeling the almost invisible growth of strings, like a gossamer web, woven by a spider at midnight? Or feeling, at least, that Willum had grown unaccountably more fond of me, not less, after finally possessing me in the back seat of my car, and other places. Doesn't it usually go the other way?

Just for fun. I wonder if anything in my life after the orchard has been just for fun. Like after the sad poem on the bench. Hayley and I pulled ourselves together and walked down to the pond and swam, but almost didn't because guess who thought the place belonged to him and him alone? Mr. Beaver. He was gigantic. Beaversaurus. He was swimming along the far edge with a stick in his mouth when he saw us, and he slapped his tail hard and made us both jump. We watched him in a kind of disbelief as he swam straight at us on the bank, and halfway there slapped his tail again and dove. He clambered out dripping and dark on the far side and glared at us.

"Hey!" Hayley yelled. "This is Lake Frith! You are welcome to swim with us, but you've gotta be nice and share!"

He blinked. He held the stick crosswise in his mouth and seemed to consider.

"I frigging mean it!" Hayley yelled.

I believe that animals have way more intelligence than we ever give them credit for, often surpassing our own. In any event, he seemed to get it. He trundled over the bank and after that we often saw him, but he never had the same attitude. We all swam together for the rest of the summer. He built a dam and a lodge in the brook, and I don't know why he clambered up to the pond to swim, but I like to think it was because he enjoyed the company.

I lay the phone back down on the desk and let it hum until it can't hum anymore. I am proud of myself. Willum, who is waxed smooth, clavicle to toe, has a rugged-looking four-wheel-drive Jeep with a shovel and a jack strapped to the roof rack. Does he even know how to use them? Probably. I'm certain he could make it here through the storm. Machismo without hair, how charming; almost irresistible. But I resist. If truth is heartbreak and life is loss, I knew how terribly easy it would be to fill the sadness with Willum. And how, right now, I'm pretty sure that would be the wrong thing to do.

Eleven

I have thought a lot about the people who approach us in our lives, those for whom we open the door, those we meet on the porch or in the yard, those we turn away. Each one is an offering, and some we accept. Mom and I accepted Rosie from the outset. We all played horseshoes, and she became part of our family without effort. Seamlessly. Like one of her tapestries on her loom: The scenes of her own life appeared over, and in, the strings of our warp. The shuttle of her being flew back and forth, and behold, we appeared, Hayley and I, in hills of green and flowers like snow, and she was with us, and the hawk of her protection flew over. No seam, no graft, no scar.

Sci-Fi roared up the hill on a regular basis with Ben, in an oversize bike helmet, clinging to his waist. He also brought gifts of venison, and a handmade knife with an antler handle.

One morning Hayley said, "C'mon, Pup, we've gotta go see the boys and reciprocate."

I looked at her, I guess blankly.

"Reciprocate? It means when somebody gives you something, you give something back."

"Because it's the right thing to do."

"Because it keeps the world turning. It's how you nurture friends and live an honorable life." She held up one finger. She did that sometimes when she knew she was lecturing.

"Oh," I said. "We're gonna see Sci-Fi?"

"Yep. We're gonna bring him a gallon of maple syrup."

I wondered if that was going overboard; we had only two. So the three of us loaded up with our can of syrup and trundled down Tavern Hill. At the stop sign we idled and Hayley ground into first gear and we were about to take off when we heard a loud rumble and then a roar and four motorcycles came fast around the bend from the Putney side, our right. I remember how they were in two staggered pairs that lengthened out at the curve and re-formed on our straightaway just the way ducks do. They thundered past, big bearded men in black leather like the Raiders, except for one who was younger and had narrow wraparound shades.

Hayley craned her neck around as they roared past.

"Fuck," she said. "Diablos. Another gang."

The four motorcycles banged and backfired as they downshifted and turned in at the Raiders' driveway.

"How do you know?" I said. Bear was whining behind us.

"Their colors."

"What's that?"

"Jackets. The big patches."

She turned off the engine. The Raiders' clubhouse was hidden by a screen of trees, but we could hear the lower idle of the bikes, and then we heard shouting and then a bang. Three more. Then four, all together. Like the shots we heard during hunting season last fall but almost in our ears. Then we heard the cough and roar of motors, and three of the Diablos thundered past us again, heading back toward Putney and the interstate. I didn't see the younger one in the wraparound shades.

Hayley's head was cocked to the side like she was listening closely to something on the wind. Maybe she was. Her neck was flushed, and when her eyes skated over me they shone with something I'd never seen before, something like fear but not exactly, something more ferocious.

"Probably just warning shots," she said finally. "Or backfires." They didn't sound like backfires. I could see the throb of the vein in her slender neck. She turned the key and started the engine and we lurched out onto the paved county road and she swung us into a U-turn and we drove home. I know now that she was protecting me, us. Whatever happened behind those trees couldn't be undone, and the Raiders didn't need any witnesses.

*

So Sci-Fi would bring Ben up to the orchard. I liked Ben fine. He was short for his age, a little smaller than me, and he usually looked bewildered. No matter what we did. I taught him to fish with a spinning rod and he threw the lure across the pond as if he was trying to hit a home run, and he always waited too long to reel in, as if he'd forgotten what to do next, and the lure would snag on the bottom. I tried to make him a captain in the army of Frith, but he never knew what to do. I gave him a sword and he broke the stick right away against our favorite apple tree and then frowned at it, dismayed. He was pretty good at horseshoes, so we often stuck to that, but I got bored after a while. He never said much, but I know he loved being in my company. I guess that was enough. I tolerated him and, oddly, I grew to miss him if he didn't show up for a week. His mom was in jail, and Sci-Fi was often gone during the day, running his motorcycle all over the state. But he usually brought venison in his backpack, and one day he showed up with a cord of firewood in the back of his truck. Hayley tried to refuse it, but he looked at the ground and I thought he would cry. "Can't use it," he said. "No stove."

"You cut the wood," Hayley said, "and don't have a woodstove?"

He didn't say anything, but he wouldn't look up. "Well, shoot," she said. "We better unload it. Thank you, Sci. Thank you very much."

The little biker never went beyond these offerings: wood, venison, and Ben a few days a week. I have wondered since if he had a crush on Hayley, or if he was just happy to make a connection for Ben, whose life, I think, was otherwise friendless. At school, during my one-day-a-week drop-in, Ben kept to himself and he was too shy to approach me on the playground or at my desk. I kept mostly to myself too. It was like our friendship could operate only at a certain altitude, which was a thousand feet up from the village and the river bottom.

In the beginning, when I showed up that first fall, I was treated as a curiosity, a novelty, and I was tested a few times by a group of girls who made a point of playing kickball and not including me—"Frith doesn't even know how to play!"—but when it became evident that it didn't bother me as it would other children, they stopped trying to get a rise out of me and left me alone. One girl, Allison Knockwood—I still remember that name—watched me drawing scenes of Viking ships and asked me if I wanted an oatmeal cookie, and after that we ate our lunches together and she invited me to her house on the Dummerston Road, where her father was a cheesemaker. When I think of her, the memory is inseparable from the smell of Aiken Brook asiago. I think that, even then, I was just going through the motions of friendship, doing what I thought I was supposed to do with another girl my age, and that the whole time a part of me would rather have been back up West Hill at the orchard, sitting on Bear and commanding my domain, or playing horseshoes with Rosie and Hayley, fishing with Ben and Mr. Beaver, or even just sharing the bench with Mom and drinking lemonade and musing on a curious world.

Is it good to be that attached to a place? Maybe it's neither good nor bad.

*

It would be good to have Willum come by later, wouldn't it? The snow has lightened, I can see it in the patio lights, drifting softly. He would not be battling a blizzard on his way over. The plows have no doubt gotten a start on the highways; he could run his Jeep happily over the back roads, plumes of powder flying up in his taillights like the wake of a fast boat.

I think of my quilts, the warmth of them, of his smooth, hard body sliding beneath, of his bashfulness in my presence. How he will do anything I ask. Tempting on a snowy night. He is not bashful, he is in awe. He has no idea that his infatuation with this quirky professor has nothing to do with love. He's a decent and sweet man, very smart, funny, self-deprecating—as well-read as almost anyone I know. He even makes fun of himself for cutting the crust off his bread and eating his sandwiches with a fork.

*

The translators' conference was in Jackson Hole. I asked Hayley why it was called that, and she explained that out west a hole can be a valley or river bottom tucked between mountains or the walls of a canyon. Jackson became known among fur trappers in the early 1800s as a sheltered valley nestled between two ranges of mountains, one of which, the Tetons, is one of the most beautiful ranges on earth.

"More beautiful than here?"

"God, no, Pup, just different."

"How?"

"I could show you a picture; they're on the conference catalog they sent me. But it might be better to be surprised."

I swung my legs, brushing the top of Bear's head, and thought about that. I could be surprised right now.

"I always found it's better to see stuff, really amazing stuff, in person. I mean for the very first time. Don't you?"

"Yep," I said, not really sure what I was agreeing to.

"Like when I went to Europe for the first time. I was invited to a conference at Vincennes, on the east edge of Paris. A big deal. I'd seen pictures of Paris, of course, but knew nothing of this place, which I'd heard had a famous castle—at one time it was the tallest building in all of France."

"A castle?" I sat up.

"Unh-huh. It's where Henry V died and where the Marquis de Sade was locked in a little room for years—" I perked up. I thought I remembered that the Marquis de Sade invented penicillin. This sounded like a place I had to see. "—and I made a point of not finding any photos. So that when I arrived and stood before it, I was without any preconceptions, and it blew me away."

"It did?"

"Yep. And you could climb up the tower, up these circular stone stairs with narrow slit windows every so often out of which you could look over the Bois de Vincennes, the great forest, and search for advancing armies." This was cool. "And on one level there was the king's chamber, kind of a little study where he used to sit by the crackling hearth with a book, or the documents of his kingdom—"

"And a flagon of mead!" I said.

"Probably."

We slid together on the bench. She said, "So what if I'd seen the pics of the castle before I went? I wouldn't have been nearly so impressed. I would have denied myself that gift. Which I will never forget."

I thought about that. How denying one gift gives you another, supposedly better. Again I thought how the world of grown-ups is a little too complicated.

*

I *was* surprised. Hayley told me she knew I would dig out the catalog, so she hid it.

On a Thursday morning in late June just after sunrise, Rosie picked us up in her Subaru. She had agreed on the spot to accompany us and be my tour guide and fishing companion over the three days while Hayley conferenced. She said she loved Jackson. And the man who ran the conference agreed to pay my plane ticket after Hayley called and explained our circumstances—single mom, etc. Hayley was never shy about asking for what she needed from the world, and I think it's because she would have been perfectly happy to stay home. Note to self.

Bill the Buyer had offered to house-sit Bear. We were in the co-op, buying our weekly staples, and he flew out from the back. He always did that when he saw us. He loved us. We were kindred souls somehow, maybe he sensed that we, like him, were in some way refugees. He asked what we were up to, and I blurted that we were going to Jackson Hole, but we didn't know what to do with Bear because Rosie was coming too. Mom thumped me.

"Sorry," Hayley said to Bill. "That wasn't a solicitation."

"I can do it," he said. "I like Bear so much." He did. We always left him leashed outside the store under a sign with rings that said DOG PARKING, and Bill always made a point of coming out with dog treats shaped like bones. Bear got so whenever he caught sight of Bill, he stood and smiled and went nuts with his tail. So they were already buddies.

Rosie picked us up just as an orange sun swam up over the shoulder of Monadnock, and we roller-coastered down the washboarded West Hill Road in the half light of the fully leafed-out forest and on into the village. We stopped for coffee and hot cinnamon rolls at the General Store—hot chocolate for me, with real whipped cream—and pulled onto Interstate 91. This was already fun. The cool morning air rushed through the open windows, and the sloping hayfields on our right, to the west, glowed with early sun. I was excited. This was our first trip by plane, across the country. I'd done it once, almost two years ago, but that was leaving. Leaving the possibility of Pop, leaving our life in Denver. That was more like flight. This was an adventure.

Airports have a smell of nervous energy and boredom. Excitement and transition, remorse, sadness. Coffee and electricity, fast-food grills, deodorant, and the sweat it can't hide. Stand in an airport sometime and try to parse the odors, it's educational. Everybody is out of their routine, a little exhausted, expectant, moving in an invisible mist of their last goodbyes. Or the smoke of their departures, if they've burned their bridges. It got to me then and it has ever since. I stand in the concourse or terminal, nostrils flaring, feeling what it's like to stand on a springboard. Nobody knows, of course, after the leap and plunge, what awaits. What will happen in the strange neighborhoods, at the family reunion, in the office towers of another city or country. In the arms of a lover not touched for too long. Nobody knows.

I was certainly jumping out of my seat when we flew low over a forested ridge into a wide green valley and there were the Tetons out my little window, swathed in snow, and rugged and towering and looking like nothing so much as the cover of *The Hobbit*, one of my favorite books. And I was jumping down the grated metal steps onto the tarmac and inhaling the high-mountain air that was so clean and sharp with sage and spruce and snow and wind. Hayley had to yell after me, "Pup! Pup! You slow down, you little maniac!"

Was I a maniac? Probably. There was something radically different about this place, something to me seemingly unearthly, maybe just in the scale of it—those mountains were gigantic! And steep! The sheer wall of them! And the valley was so flat and grassy-wide, nothing like back home. And the sky held a thousand high white clouds that could not come close to obscuring it. Andandand.

I fell head over heels. The great American West, in the very first moments, picked me up and shook me the way Bear liked to shake his ratty plush squirrel and challenged me ever to be the same. I never was. It's a wonder I didn't angle for a teaching gig in Denver, as Mom did, or Boise or Salt Lake.

We got our bags off the conveyor—Hayley had to yank me off it when I tried to ride someone's duffel like a pony—and Rosie got her rental-car keys from the counter and we walked out into the thin sunlight and the buffeting wind so full of those tangy smells. We found the four-wheel-drive in the parking lot. It was boxy and shiny black. That was novel; no one back in Putney had a black car. We drove into town. I opened the window and stuck my head out, into the wind, the way Bear did from the back of the truck, so that I had to squint hard to keep my hair from whipping my eyeballs. I couldn't keep them off those mountains.

"Hey!" I yelled over the wind. "Can we climb that tall one?"

"Probably not!" Rosie yelled.

"Why not?" I screamed.

"Because!" Hayley hooted. "It's like ten times higher than Putney Mountain!"

"So what!"

"It's got cliffs and snow and ice! And grizzly bears!"

"So!"

"So, get back into your seatbelt!"

I wished Bear could have been here. I knew he would stick his head out right beside mine and go nuts with the new everything.

The hotel was made of logs, so we felt right at home, and it was right across the street from the art center where Hayley would have her conference. It had only three stories and an elevator, which seemed extravagant. The young women at the front desk wore snap western shirts and Wranglers and cowboy boots, and big silver buckles.

"Are you a cowgirl?" I asked the one who had asked our names. "Or is this like Pioneer Village?" Pioneer Village was in New Hampshire, near Keene, and it had men in tricorn hats and women in white caps who made candles and everybody was fake.

She was blond and pretty and her face brightened, and she laughed. "What's your name?" she said.

"Frith."

"That's one I've never heard. It's pretty."

"Yep," I said. "It's from *The Snow Goose.*"

She blinked. She'd never heard of it. "Cool."

She stuck out her slender hand and I shook it. I knew she wasn't a real cowgirl then because her hand was smooth and she had fuchsia nail polish. A real cowgirl's hands would be more like Hayley's.

Rosie got her own room, though we'd invited her to share ours. Our room had two beds, so we made one for laying out clothes and jumping on. There was a little balcony that looked over a leafy brook and the grass ski slopes of a mountain. I'd never been skiing, but we could see the trails of Stratton and Mount Snow from the top of Putney Mountain. Hayley promised she'd take me in the coming winter.

Hayley had a reception dinner in a few hours, so we figured we'd just walk the town. We started with our neighborhood near the hotel. Most of the houses had only one story, most had flower and vegetable gardens, a lot had snowshoes and old skis and stuff nailed over the doors and wind spinners on the fences, and a bunch had little boats on trailers parked in the driveways or on the street. Hayley told us they were drift-boats and skiffs for fishing.

"Fishing!"

"Yes," she said. "That's a big thing around here. Fly-fishing, like I taught you, with the little tufts of fur and feathers."

"Cool!"

"In the summer everybody fishes. Like us. In the winter they ski."

"Sounds like The Life," I said.

We worked our way toward the center of town, and as we did, the streets got more and more crowded, until we were on the cowboy boardwalks that ran in front of the fancy shops and restaurants and we had to jostle single file, and then we got to the square with the big gates made out of elk antlers. Everybody was taking snapshots there.

We asked a Chinese family to take our picture, and I was amazed to see the mother bow. Not from the waist, not deep, but definitely a bow. I made Ben bow to me when we played Vikings, but mostly he forgot and got on his knees, not one knee like I taught him. This was the first time I'd ever seen anyone do it for real, uncoerced.

We got soft-serve ice cream cones from a truck on the corner, and we sat in a line on a bench in the shade of the big, leafy trees. When the wind blew, it cooled the sweat on our necks and the trees loosed a snow of fluff. Rosie told me they were the seeds of the cottonwoods, which was why they were called that.

This *was* The Life. I really liked being a tourist.

When we finished our cones, we walked back to the hotel. Hayley had to get ready for her dinner. On the way, we passed a jewelry store with a lot of silver in the window and Hayley said, "Let's go in for a sec." I didn't get past the first glass case. I'd never been in a jewelry store. Hayley never wore jewelry, she wore only the gold wedding band Pop had given her and which she never took off, even when we moved to the orchard. I was dazzled, I admit.

The whole cabinet was silver with opaque blue stones. Rosie told me they were turquoise. Mrs. Kreutzer, my second-grade teacher at the school, wore a tiny diamond ring, and when I asked her about it, she told me proudly that it was her engagement ring. And since then I'd kept an eye out for engagement rings. Whenever we went into town I looked at women's hands, and I had cataloged sapphires, diamonds, emeralds, even rubies. Diamonds I didn't get; they looked like chips of glass. If I ever made a real queen's crown, I vowed to leave them out, why waste the space? Emeralds I could definitely get used to. But this turquoise took the cake. Some were the color of the sky in the morning on a clear day, some were milky, some were green like the quarry, and I liked how they looked like real stones, not colored glass. There were bracelets with rows of stones, heavy pendants, slender earrings. I loved them all.

"Stop drooling," Rosie said and poked me.

I wiped my mouth. "I'm not drooling!"

"You want to."

"Okay," Hayley said briskly. "Let's go." She pulled us toward the front door, and I noticed she carried a little paper bag with tiny handles.

When we got to our rooms, Hayley yanked off her top and bra and rinsed her face in the sink and said, "Whew! Being a tourist is exhausting, isn't it, Pup?"

"It's awesome."

She shook her mass of curls and gathered them back off her neck and fanned herself with her hair. "Air-conditioning," she said.

"I don't like it. It's like living inside our little fridge."

"I know." She went to the unit by the sliding door that opened onto the balcony and shut it off, and she slid open the door and let the breeze and the new smells in, and the sound of the stream. "Better." Then she reached out to the countertop by the big TV and handed me the paper bag. Inside was a small box wrapped in a blue ribbon. "For you," she said.

I yanked the ends of the bow and lifted the lid, and lying on a bed of cotton was a turquoise pendant on a thin silver chain. It was a deep blue-green, the color of the pond in the long light of evening, at the hour just before the sun dropped over the woods behind us, over Putney Mountain. It was shaped a little like the pond too, more oblong than round, and it was held in a simple silver bezel.

"Put it on," she said. "I'll help you. The clasp takes a little getting used to." I think I was paralyzed. She came behind me and reached around and lifted the chain from the box until the pendant swung free and she whispered, "Lift your hair," and I did. I felt her rough, confident fingers brush the nape of my neck.

"There," she said, and she let the pendant fall. It lay against my breastbone beneath my clavicle, where it has lain to this day. I've had to get two chains since.

*

Hayley got dressed that evening as I'd never seen her. A blue satin pencil skirt and black sandals with heels. Bouncing curls and earrings of dangling silver bells she got in Peru. Lipstick. She was a knockout. A different animal, but still Hayley, still with the spray of freckles across her nose unobscured by concealer. Still the muscular tan hands.

Maybe it was the contrasts that had the men looking, because I noticed that they kept turning back. Wow, my mom. It was the rareness of her, the vitality, the whiff of the orchard, sun, dirt, woodsmoke, and . . . this, this gorgeous woman. She was a force, for sure. We walked her to the reception, which was only a block away and across the street, and in that short stretch, half a dozen heads turned, men and women. I felt proud. That's my mom! I wanted to tell them all.

Rosie turned heads too, I noticed, after we dropped Mom off and the two of us walked back toward the plaza and the center of town. But the looks had a different tenor. A sideways glance, a quiet nod of appreciation. She was in jeans and zipped half boots and her mass of sunny hair swung on her shoulders, and she had a natural ruddiness from spending time outside. But with her frameless glasses, and the cool reserve she carried with her the way a mountain makes its own weather, it was she who seemed the intellectual, the studious one.

The sun had tipped below the ridge, and the air instantly cooled. The sidewalks were less crowded, and I remember walking with her and feeling privileged. Rich. For one, we didn't have to worry about where dinner was going to come from. Hayley and I often had to get creative and stretch whatever we had; sometimes we'd catch a mess of brook trout just to add protein to the noodles. Walking with Rosie, I felt again how we were a unit, we were relaxed, we engaged the world as it flowed by us, just the way the trout did, swimming slowly up an eddy line.

We decided the center of town had too much hubbub and we circled back and ate on the patio of a Mexican restaurant from where we could see, over the rooftops, a wooded ridge whose top half was still lit with sunlight. It was the first time I'd had Mexican food and Rosie ordered me horchata, the sweet rice milk drink, which I sucked down, and chiles rellenos, which might have been the best thing I'd ever eaten—until I bit into the fresh, fried-dough pillow of a sopaipilla covered in honey. I'd had no idea that food could be this fun. Why didn't people eat this stuff at every meal, seven days a week?

Rosie cut pieces of carne asada covered in green chile and dropped them on my plate. The novel touch of the turquoise pendant bouncing against my skin; also the pleasure of displaying something precious and beautiful, which was new. And knowing Mom was a few blocks away, being the belle of the ball. That sense of fullness, bounty. It wasn't the first time I'd felt it, but this was a different animal.

Twelve

The next couple of days were startling in that the onslaught of thrills may have actually exceeded even the imagination of Frith.

Hayley met us in the lobby after ten that night, and she was ablaze. I'd never seen her so lit up, which made me a little jealous, and I'm pretty certain it wasn't just the wine. The lobby of our log hotel was like someone's huge living room, and we all sat in a nook on a leather couch by a stone hearth. The night was chilly, the stars out in full force. Rosie and I had just come back from sitting on one of the grass slopes of Snow King, which is what the ski mountain was called, where we'd traced out and named every constellation we could see. I was wearing the pendant and also the soft wool hoodie Rosie had knit for me. And now we were all together by this fireplace where a wood fire crackled. Hayley talked exuberantly of sitting next to W. S. Merwin, whose eyes, she said, were so intelligent and spaced so far apart he looked like a whale. Robert Pinsky had told her a Vermont joke about a farmer and a counterfeiter that made her laugh and laugh. Everybody knew, had read, *Poems of Tsu Mountain*. So the bounty was added to and rippled out from our little family unit.

The next day, Rosie took me horseback riding out in the valley, where we could see that wall of snowy mountains. My first time on a horse. The young woman who led us was not like the ones at the hotel. She wore a battered fawn cowboy hat and dusty boots and her hands were tendoned like Hayley's, and she swung up into the saddle and spun her horse and whistled like a cowboy in a movie. I was awestruck, and nearly swapped Nordic Queen for Wyoming Cowgirl on the spot. Fickle Frith. On Saturday, Rosie took me fishing—in a raft, on the Snake, right beneath those mountains. It had been a late, cool spring, and the river was high but not too high. Hayley had taught me to throw a dry fly, and I'd caught brookies that way back in the orchard, but that day I caught my first fish on a nymph—a twenty-inch golden brown trout. Under the instruction of Nate, the skinny, stooped, shy guide whom I kept trying to shoehorn into the story of Mom with Pop in the bayou. I was awestruck again, a little crushed, as in having a crush.

Rosie was a surprisingly good rider. It seemed it was something she must have done all her life, but she didn't brag about it. But when we fished, she demurred. Her grandfather had taught her to fish in South Carolina, bass fishing with poppers in the slow tannin rivers, and she loved it. I asked her why she didn't want to fish that day—Nate had extra rods—and she put her chin in her hand and leaned forward and said, "Sometimes you leave things with the people you did them with."

“You mean you don’t do it anymore because you can’t do it with your grandfather?”

“Right. Not everything. Just certain special things. I don’t know why.”

“Huh,” I said. Then I turned to my new boyfriend on the oars and said, “Okay, Nate, that looks like fishy water! Where should I throw it?”

The days passed like that.

On Sunday afternoon, Rosie and I got back to the hotel after driving up into Yellowstone and seeing a grizzly bear with two cubs romping around at the edge of a field. Hayley was lying on our bed when I burst into the room. She had a hand towel over her eyes.

“Hi hi!” I called. “We saw a bear! Three! Then we had Shirley Temples at the Cowboy Bar, they have real saddles for stools!”

“Hi, Pup,” she said. I stopped by the bathroom. Her voice was a monotone and it came from a distance. Her short black business skirt was on the floor.

“What’s wrong?” I said.

“You mind getting me a glass of water? There are glasses to the right of the TV.”

I knew where they were. “Sure.” I filled one up in the bathroom sink. “Here.”

"Thanks, sweetheart. You can just put it down." Her voice almost as if heard underwater. She never called me sweetheart. This was bad. In all our struggles together, I'd never seen her like this.

Rosie tapped and breezed in; we'd given her an extra key. "Hey," she called. "Hayle! How was the radio interview?" She stopped as I had.

"Oh," she said. She needed no explanation. "Bad, huh? Something happened."

Short nod on the bed.

"You wanna talk about it?"

Silence.

"You wanna get an early dinner? Maybe go to the Greek place in the Jackson Hotel?"

Silence.

"I . . ." Hayley said, finally. And then she coughed. Hard. It racked her whole body, which jumped with muscles. Her hands came to her mouth and she coughed into them, trying to muffle it. The little towel slid off her face, and I saw the light tracks of salt on her temples where her tears had run.

"Whew, sorry." Her faint croak. I had never heard her apologize for being herself. Rosie was at her side, sitting on the margin of the bed. One long weaver's hand covered Mom's and the other was dabbing at her mouth and cheeks with the towel, which I now saw was wet.

"What on earth happened?" Rosie said.

"It's why I got out of this . . . this business," Mom said.

"What?"

"The interview . . ." Her eyes fluttered open and found each of us. She attempted a smile, failed. "My big interview. With Clarissa Stenn." Whoever she was. "Live."

"Yeah?"

"It was fine for the first ten minutes." She wheezed, cleared her throat. "She asked about Li Xue, her life, her exile. Then she said, 'So why, in the age of feminism, do we need ancient Chinese poems which recapitulate the male gaze?' "

"What?"

"I know," Mom murmured. "I was confused too. I said, 'They don't recapitulate the male gaze. Li Xue is a woman. Very much so. These poems are all written by a woman, one of the greatest poets of the Tang dynasty.'

" 'Sure,' she said. 'Of course. But don't you agree that, while she is a great stylist, she is merely enacting and reinforcing a male fantasy? Namely, standing at the window, crying, and waiting for her man to come home?' Something like that. I was flabbergasted. I could tell she had rehearsed this, that this was what the interview was about, she had led me along and then *slam*!

"I felt ambushed, panicked. I stuttered, I think, started to answer, backed up. All the time she was looking at me like a wolf. Oh, God—"

She coughed again, racked her body, waved away the towel. She sat up, huffed out a clean breath, looked at us both. "I'm really glad to see you guys."

"God, what a nightmare," Rosie said. "So what happened?"

"I tried. I mean, in the rush of panic I was thinking, *I've come such a long way to be here, this is really unfair.* And then I thought, *No, Hayley, this is part of the job. This is a clean debate, intellectual rigor and all that.* And then I thought, *No no no no! This is just why I left this frigging world. Why we moved to the orchard in the first place. Because of this stuff! The cruelty! The ego!* And then I thought, *Get your shit together and answer the mean lady.*"

I was on the edge of my seat. This story had a David and Goliath quality, and it was starring my favorite person. I sat on the bed at her bare feet and squeezed her toes, one at a time, I don't know why.

"Did you let her have it?" I said. "Chapter and verse?"

Mom's sideways, half-surprised look—like, *Is that my child again, saying surprising stuff?* She was back, the old Hayley. Phew.

"I said, 'I beg your pardon, but Li Xue happens to be an aficionado of loss. She writes about loss and heartbreak as few other writers ever have, man or woman. With honesty and directness, in a style so sophisticated and elegant, so deceptively simple, many readers will see only powerful nature poems. And love them for just that. Most of the poetry of the Tang, the entire catalog, from Li Shimin to Yu Xuanji, is about loss, as I said. Loss of home, loss of a friend, loss of a lover. Loss of youth, of life itself. Male and female poets alike, that's what they write about.'

"She rolled right over my defense and said the next line she had practiced: 'I mean, okay, Li Xue is a great poet. But isn't that like saying so-and-so is a top porn actress? Fantastic at what she does, granted, but all in the service of the male-gratification industry? Waiting for her man and crying. I mean, why do we need this? You are a skilled translator, why bend your skills, your prodigious intellect, to these plaints? Isn't that kind of a sellout?'

"Kind of a sellout. I had no answer. I struggled to breathe myself. How could she say that? Any of it? Li Xue was pure and honest, so was Li Bai, so was Du Fu. Some of the greatest poets the universe has ever produced. I guess I began to dissociate. I think the last thing I stammered was 'I translate the poems because I love them. . . .' Then I felt myself lift out of my body. Like a spirit. I lifted out and up and I was looking down at myself and at her in the little sound studio, the two of us with headphones, leaning into the spongy mics.

"I heard her laugh uncomfortably. Like she was far away, and she was saying something like 'Well, we certainly didn't mean to put you on the spot, way out here under the jagged spires of the Tetons! This has been a remarkable conference, stimulating, invigorating, even contentious at times! This is Clarissa Stenn for *The Nation* and WGBH in Boston, signing off . . .' "

I don't know if I myself was breathing. This was not the ending I had imagined. Goliath didn't seem to be knocked out with a stone.

Thirteen

The memory clenches my heart. I make myself lift the still-hot cup of Lapsang and drink, make myself taste the smoke, the swirl of sweetness in the honey. Make myself open my eyes to the tapering storm, the light drift of snow beyond the glass, the flakes that could almost be a flurry of cottonwood fluff. The past is close tonight but cannot change the present, not now. Or can it?

I breathe. I shuffle my hands through the remaining pages of poems, turn over the one on top.

"Summer Evening," to the tune of "Hawthorn Blossoms."

A happy poem, presumably. Because Hayley did not curl up. My mother had grit. She went right back to translating Li Xue, and if anything, the lantern burned longer into the night; and she read and sang back softly the lines with more intensity.

They—the *they* that was more than Clarissa Stenn or some conference, but was all of academia, the top-heavy mass of it, and all of those driven by not-love for what they did, or not-love of others—they were an entire society that could not slow down enough to remember the power in a simple truth.

To Hayley, that truth was simply seeing. Seeing with honesty and clarity; making oneself still enough, vulnerable enough, to encounter an other fully. Here, the other was Li Xue. They would not shove my mother off her path with politics. God, no. It was exactly why the poetess of Chang'an had left the capital for the country, for her own dilapidated farm on the Yellow River.

I watched Hayley from the loft, late into the night, later than I used to, because I was fascinated by the intensity with which she returned to the place she felt safe. Maybe safety wasn't it—it was where she felt most at home, I think. Where she gathered and garnered her strength, straight from the words of a woman I was beginning to think of as her doppelgänger, though I wouldn't have known the word.

So:

Summer Evening

Is there anything more lovely than the glide of the current
when the sun has settled beyond Tsu Mountain?
Or the shadowy flight of the herons returning one by one to the trees?

Someone is playing "Waterlilies and Fireflies" patiently on ten strings.
We light the candles in the western pavilion.
Is there anything we have not said to each other? I cannot tell
anymore whose poems are whose.

Nobody knows by what path she will arrive at the Golden Palace.
Tonight as we pour out the wine I am happy to hum the words,
to lean our heads together,
to leave thoughts of the Silver Bridge to another season.
Before moonrise maybe she will play "Hawthorn Blossoms."

A happy poem, yes. Of friendship, it seems. Tinged with sadness, with impending loss. A looking back and a looking forward. She is happy to leave thoughts of death until fall, when poets cannot help themselves, or until winter, maybe; but she confesses on this lovely summer night that the thoughts are with her, she cannot forestall them.

What we do, some of us, when the bounty of our lives flows over. We almost cannot bear the beauty, and our thoughts turn to the inevitable end.

Maybe that's comforting—when the beauty overwhelms. The love of our lives on a peaceful summer evening, the love of a friend. When we feel cradled by the universe. To know that it will end, it must. The simple reckoning that might help us somehow accept it all.

Hayley bent to the string of ancient characters, the English words gathering to their right like so many bees humming to a hedge of flowers. She bent in the light of the lantern, which gleamed on the chestnut of her hair, the two strands of silver. And she coughed, a hard, merciless cough that convulsed her shoulders. She coughed into folded arms, and when she was done, she shook her head as if dispelling a bad dream. She stood from the table, shaken. I wanted to scoot back on the bed in the loft, to hide myself, but I was incapable of movement. She walked to the sink, reaching one hand to the plank counter to steady herself, which reminded me of Rosie's Aunt Marie. She turned the tap and the cabin refilled with a comforting sound, the musical thrub of cold spring water hitting the bottom of the steel sink. She took a coffee cup off the shelf above, filled it, drank all of it in one go, cleared her throat gingerly so as not to start up another spasm. Filled it, drank again.

I watched from the loft, chin over the edge of the bed, unable to move or speak. I was held tight, in the grip of an unspoken knowledge that a shadow was moving over our lives. Just the way the sadness permeates this poem. The way it slows the soft repetitions of the lute, the summer night, the wordless tune called "Waterlilies and Fireflies."

*

By August the coughing got so bad Rosie insisted Hayley see Dr. Dixon in Brattleboro. I was to find out later that we did not have regular health insurance—there was no way Hayley could have afforded it—but she did pay for a cheap, high-deductible catastrophic plan to protect me in case I was struck with some terrible childhood disease—which she was certain, knowing my feisty constitution, would never happen—or some disastrous accident—which, knowing my feisty constitution, she thought was a possibility. What she never anticipated was that she would get sick. In college she had smoked. In grad school, when she began to dive deeply into translation and was transported wholly into other eras, into mountain ranges twice as tall as any she had ever seen, and wars with nomadic armies, she began to smoke more. One detail that had not made it into the story of her meeting Johnny Cormier was that, as they shared their fish fillet sandwiches, tied up in the shade of the tupelo at the edge of a lake, they shared a pack of Marlboro Reds. When she got pregnant with me she quit, went cold turkey the very day she found out. But. She had smoked, sometimes heavily, for years.

Hayley did not have the money to see Dr. Dixon, I overheard her telling Rosie the first time I ever heard their voices raised against each other. Four of us were playing horseshoes, Hayley and I against Rosie and Ben. It was a heavy August afternoon, a low sky threatening rain, humid, still, with that long light that gleams off the leaves in the way it does only in August.

We'd finished our delivery of beignets and po'boys all over West Hill. That was Hayley's latest scheme: to make Cajun lunch baskets and deliver them fresh to the kitchens and home offices scattered up Tavern Hill and Putney Mountain and across Dusty Ridge.

They were wildly popular. For the price of a sandwich and soda down at the deli in the General Store or at the co-op, one could have a picnic basket delivered, neatly filled with a Louisiana po'boy—sometimes we had a choice of specials stuffed with Sci-Fi's venison or trout we caught from the brook, none of it maybe strictly legal—a still-hot beignet, and a sweating Dr Pepper. Kind of like a Cajun bento box. We got to know all our neighbors, and they were taken immediately, of course, with the two of us in our overalls and unruly hair, mother and daughter, often humming, in our claptrap truck, bouncing up to hand-deliver a lunch that brightened their day with tastes that, for the Puritan New England hills, were leaning toward the exotic. And the baskets were traditional woven picnic baskets Hayley got for a song down at Basketville, Putney's only import-warehouse-slash-tourist-attraction. One of the owners gave her a deal because she had several hundred of the things and they weren't moving, as they were really too small for a traditional picnic. We'd drop a basket off and pick up the empty. Hayley was single-handedly responsible for getting a good slice of Putney addicted to Dr Pepper.

Well, it kept us in chicken feed and dog food and cheese fondue—my favorite meal after Mexican.

We had completed our round of deliveries and were enjoying the wonderful respite that comes when you have finished the job and still have a long summer afternoon ahead. I loved that feeling. And we felt rich. Florence Watts had given us half a blueberry pie she made the day before, and Hy Kyung Brandt, the shy and lovely wife of the Korea scholar who lived at the end of the West Hill Road, had said, "Wait, just for a minute," and she'd gone back inside the cedar-shingled house and returned with a folded silk robe in a pattern of tiny roses, in my size. I wore it every night afterwards, until I grew out of it.

We were rich now, but not rich enough apparently.

On that overcast afternoon with the crickets and peepers thrumming, Hayley and I were beating Rosie and Ben, which was rare, and Hayley had just thrown a leaner, which, with the small shoes, was probably harder than a ringer, and I was jumping up and down, and she began to cough. She coughed so hard she had to sit down on the low boulder, and when she finally finished and caught her breath, she wiped something off her hand which I knew was blood. And then she said, "Just a sec, I'll get some lemonade for everyone," and she walked slowly up the steps. Rosie went after her, and I could hear her pleading with Mom inside the cabin to go to the doctor.

"It's time," she said. "You need to see someone." Rosie said it louder than she needed to, and I know it was because she was scared.

"Stay out of it," Hayley said. "Can you get the pitcher out of the fridge, please?"

"You've been putting and putting it off . . ." The rising voice. "You can't do that anymore! You're really sick!"

"I love you dearly, but please stay the fuck out of it." Her own strained voice, which could not carry the volume and cracked again.

More coughing. Apologies and pleading from Rosie. Eventually, the two of them, composed, coming back down the steps. An ice-fogged pitcher, four jelly jar glasses, fragile smiles.

Rosie ended up paying. She thought Mom's resistance was about money. I think that it was the fear of learning the truth. Our lives were so good now. Thoughts of the Silver Bridge could be put off to another season.

*

I flip over the next page, in a hurry now to get past my own memories.

Late Summer Cricket

There is nothing you can tell me
you have not been telling me all morning.
I know you are lonely.
Me, too.
And that though you sing and sing for love,
you are somehow happy in your loneliness.
As am I.
And that you smell rain as I do, and so you are excited
for the first patter in the maple leaves, the first trembling
grass.

Oh, God, I love this poem. It's maybe my favorite so far. There are dates, thank goodness, at the bottom of every page, right-hand corner, just a string of six tiny digits in pencil—as if the date a translation was finished might someday be revised. I don't think it ever was; I never saw signs of eraser marks. I think Hayley knew exactly when she was done with a poem. And so I know that this is one she did in those days of late August when we were delivering our Cajun picnics and driving with Rosie out to the quarry and playing horseshoes with Ben, and fishing, and we were rich, and I might have been delirious except that my mother's coughing shook the foundations of my joy.

Fourteen

Dr. Dixon is an old man now, and he is still my friend. He lives on the Dummerston Road in a tight red clapboard farmhouse beside an ancient white-painted barn, the reverse of most color schemes in northern New England. He had trained two Percherons to skid logs, and they lived in the barn, and I think the white paint was a sign of his respect. His wife was the head librarian at the Brattleboro Public Library, and he loved her so much that when she died of a sudden aneurysm, he buried her himself in his pasture and ever after went out in the evening, whatever the weather, and shared a cup of tea by her grave and told her of his day and the weather and the horses.

Hayley could not have been in better care. Dr. Dixon held her hand as he talked to her, and what he had to say was not sanguine. And she had known this. She had known she was sick. And so when he told her the truth, she did not burst into tears or beg for a second opinion or more tests. She knew. The X-rays showed the two spots on her lungs, the CT scan and the blood tests confirmed their malignancy. They did not need a biopsy; they would go in and remove the tumors.

I was with her. That was not a normal protocol, but Hayley said, "She's my partner in crime, Doc, she can be in the room." That made me proud and a little scared. When he said they would schedule as fast as possible, in just ten days, Hayley huffed out a rasped breath and said, "And then what?"

"And then chemo and radiation."

She was my mom. She looked tired and a little thinner, a little gaunt in the cheeks and around the eyes, but otherwise normal. I remember thinking: What if we just thank Dr. Dixon and walk out of here and go back to our lives? Sit on the bench on the porch and watch the swallows cut the air, and go to bed, me in the loft and her later, after bending to the table for an hour or two? And make po'boys and beignets and whistle for Bear to load up and go on our rounds in the sultry, lush late-summer afternoons? And chat with everybody along the way, and thereby bring home not only our stack of checks and dollars, but all the stories from the pasture-patched hills? Why can't we just walk out of here and let the current of our days pick us up again and carry us along as it always has before?

First stage of grief, I guess.

Hayley was not grieving. She glanced at me to make sure I was okay, and she said, "Okay, let's go. We'll give this our best shot, won't we, Pup?"

I nodded.

*

My mother, Hayley McCallister Cormier, was positively diagnosed with lung cancer on September 4. I will never forget the day, because it was the Tuesday after Labor Day. I remember we had had to wait through a week and then the long weekend to get her results.

Dr. Dixon's office was in Brattleboro, in a sturdy Victorian with a deep porch on a leafy street that ran into Main. It looked more like a B&B than a doctor's office, and Hayley said that anyone who had their office behind a porch like that probably had their priorities straight. How many diagnoses like Mom's had he delivered in that house? Too many to count. After hearing the verdict, we got Bear out of the truck and leashed him and walked down the steep hill.

"Let's stop in the bookstore and then treat ourselves to dinner," she said. "Sound like a plan?"

"Definitely." I held her left hand. She held Bear's leash with the other. We walked, tried not to let him tug us downhill. I felt privileged again, I don't know why. To be with her this way, on this day. She was not going to let me get wet, not by one drop, in the rain of her own grief or self-pity. She knew in her heart, I guess, that one day I would make plenty of weather on my own.

Do we feel the canopy thinning above us? As we grow, as our elders decline and fall? I was not ready for that, for any thinning at all. The raw sky with all its violence is too harsh without the protective shade of a parent. I may have been a Nordic Queen in my own mind, but I definitely needed a Queen Mother. Did I have an idea of the implications of what we'd just heard? Yes. I was no dummy, as I've been at pains to point out.

We just walked. We didn't say anything after that. She held my hand, and at times I felt her grip tighten on mine with the rhythm, I guess, of her own thoughts, which must have been racing. I have grit too. I did not fill the space with questions or jabber. We were complete in our own company, as we had always been. Comfortable in silence on the bench on the porch, or in the truck with the air pouring in the open windows and Bear in the back with his paws up on the wheel well and his head stuck forward grinning into the wind, or in our bed in the loft, spooning, silent.

We got to Main and turned left and walked up to Green Mountain Books, where Hayley liked to browse and once in a while treated herself. "Let's just check in here. I ordered something, let's see if it's in." The owner, Garth, revered Hayley and kept *Poems of Tsu Mountain* on a special stand on the front counter. She tied Bear to a light pole and we pushed through the red door. Garth was at his little island in the middle of the store, which we called Garth Atoll. He was reading a computer screen through granny glasses at the end of his nose, and when he heard the little bell on the door, he looked up and his face lit. He was from St. Lucia and was very proud to have known the family of Derek Walcott, and he adored poetry of all stripes.

"Look what the cat dragged in on little cat feet," he said brightly.

"Being dragged is how we feel," Hayley said.

"Yep, dragged," I said.

"Well, shoot, let's undrag you! Ginger tea?"

I looked at Hayley, who nodded.

"BTW, your book came in. Just yesterday." He reached under the counter and pulled out the new revised edition of Kenneth Rexroth's *One Hundred Poems from the Chinese.*

"You two look . . . tired," Garth said.

"We're suddenly tired," Hayley said. "How's business?"

"For a gay black man in one of the whitest places on earth, pretty good." That's what he always said.

I had always loved coming into this store with Hayley, because it was one of the few times I was reminded that she was a star. That she had done something big in her life—was doing it—aside from catering to Yours Truly. That can be a revelation to a child.

He had an electric kettle in back that was always simmering, and there was a couch back there and a couple of threadbare stuffed chairs and a fifteen-year-old Great Dane named Blue who could barely stand. I liked to curl up with him on his stinky pillow, which he never seemed to mind, so that's what I did. I forgot about the tea and I fell asleep to the two of them chatting. I'm sure it was the sleep of the traumatized. I never heard Hayley mention her diagnosis before I dropped off, and I'm sure she didn't mention it later. They talked about his new boyfriend, a philosophy professor at Northeastern, and the new poems of a transgender poet from Miami, and then Hayley was shaking me gently awake. We thanked Garth and retrieved Bear and walked farther up Main to the River House, where Hayley treated us to a fancy pork chop dinner on the veranda overlooking the slow, dark currents of the Connecticut.

*

She did not work that night at the table—it had been a long, long day—and the next morning we awoke early and walked. We walked uphill and crossed Dusty Ridge and passed Frazier's fields, which were waist high in yellowing grass and ready for the third cutting. We turned the corner at the Osgoods' house and got on a trail called Blueberries, which wound up the back side of Putney Mountain. The first bracing morning that presaged fall. Bear ran ahead, made wide circles in the woods, came back. The early sun spilled through the canopy and pattered into the ferns. I could smell them warming and begin to see at the edge of the trail, poking out of old leaves, the crimson bodies of newts. There's a time in these woods, on these hills, when walking the trails is like swimming through honey. The color, not the viscosity. It may be all the beech trees, and ash, and birch, all the trees that soften to yellows early, before the onslaught of the more brilliant colors. Some of the hedges and underbrush were already turning too. The sumacs were reddening. But the prevailing mood was something golden.

Again we didn't say much. Mom coughed a little, stopped a few times on the climb up to the old green trailer, long abandoned. It had rained hard two nights before, and the ledge rock on the steeps was slick with seeping water. I was not used to her resting on a walk; it had always been her pushing us up the mountain, me needing a break. Now, for the first time, I waited. I called Bear in. The three of us stood on a ledge and caught our breath and endured the alarmed chatter of a squirrel, the squall of a jay. And when they were done, we heard water trickling and the far-off hollow call of a barn owl that could not let go of night. Hayley smiled at me. She reached out and combed her hardened fingers through my tangled hair, tugged.

"Any birds' nests in there?"

"Probably," I said. I reached up and took her hand.

"The next few months are going to be rough," she said.

"They are?" I wouldn't look at her.

"Yes," she said. "And I'm going to give it my best shot, like I said." She wouldn't lie to me. I remember that. She didn't say we would get through it, it would all be okay.

"Okay," I said.

"We're lucky to have Rosie," she said.

"We are?" I knew we were. I was just answering now, call-and-response.

"I talked to her last night after you fell asleep. She came over for a late cup of tea."

"Oh."

"She'll be around a lot, even more. Some days she'll take you to school and stuff."

"I can bike to school." Which was true.

"I know. But when it gets really cold and when it snows and winter comes."

When winter comes.

"And she'll bring me to chemo. Us. A few days a week, and she'll bring you to visit me."

I swung my head around. "To visit you?"

"There will be times I'll be in the hospital, like next week when I have the surgery."

I looked at my mother, who'd always had enough strength for both of us. Hayley the fighter. Who was always strong, always had a plan and made it fun somehow. There was no fun now, no pretense.

"It's gonna be hard," she said.

I looked up at her. I nodded. In that spangled yellow light, her eyes were lit with green. Her freckles sprayed over her nose like always; her unruly hair. Her hair loosed a strand across her chapped lips that she now pushed back. I thought she was the strongest, most beautiful woman on earth.

Her chest rose and fell as she filled and refilled her lungs. Her eyes were steady and they held me. Bear leaned against my leg, panted, lowered his head and lapped at the black water seeping over the rock.

Fifteen

The buzzing of the phone on the desk wakes me from the memory, and I'm relieved. Outside the glass doors the snow has almost stopped. I'm relieved, but it's also hard to leave the morning trail and Hayley.

I reach for the phone because that's who I am now and turn it over and it's Willum again—well after eleven o'clock—and this time I touch the screen to answer, I don't know why.

"Hey," he says. "I've been trying to reach you."

"I know."

"Are you okay?"

"Why wouldn't I be?"

Silence, a beat. "The storm, I guess."

"It's beautiful, don't you think?"

"I guess it is. You're always so positive." Beat. "You okay? You sound funny."

"I'm fine."

He coughs lightly. "I wanted to tell you that I got a job in New York."

I straighten in my chair. Now he has my attention. "You did?"

"Yes, at Macmillan. As an assistant editor. Fiction."

"Wow, Willum, that's amazing. Congratulations. What you've wanted. Incredible."

"Yes." I can imagine him batting his eyes, blushing, as if he were here in the room.

"That's so great."

"Yes, thanks." Pause. "I was thinking. I was wondering . . ."

Now, not only am I sitting up, but my chest tightens. Almost as if an icy gust had shoved through the French doors. I have no idea what he is going to say, but I sense the gist of it. Frith is no fool.

"You could get a gig at Columbia in a heartbeat. You know you could. You're probably more famous now than your mother . . ." *Ha!* I think. *Not sure of that, but you're on a roll, Willum.*

"I've been looking already at places in Greenpoint. I . . . I would split child care with you. More, if you needed."

"How would you do that, with a full-time job?" I can't believe I'm saying that. The words surprise me.

"I talked to my mom. She has some money. She said she'd help pay for a nanny."

A nanny? Willum as an earnest dad, and presumably a husband. I'm thunderstruck. Where on earth is all this coming from? Is it the odd suspension of reality that comes with big storms?

"What brought this on?" I say, finally. "We hardly know each other."

"I don't think that's true," he shoots back.

"You don't?"

"Well." I can feel him trying to corral his thoughts and emotions. I understand in this moment that he is making himself maybe more vulnerable than he has in his entire young life.

"I've been . . . I don't know. I've been loving you for years."

I let those words ring. I do not laugh them off, good for me. I just let them sound in the half dark.

"Huh," I say. Maybe it isn't the most compassionate response. He's a good man, as far as I can tell. Decent, attentive, thoughtful. He is well-read. He certainly has a quiet sense of humor. He wants to be a dad to my child—our child.

"You want to be a father?" I say. Cut me some slack for being taken completely by surprise. Kind of like a Scottish coastal village waking to Aud's longboat grating up onto the beach.

"I want to be a father with you."

Oh, God, that is so sweet. I look down at my barely swelling belly, place a protective hand over it. I let my eyes move up to the sheaf of poems on the desk, half of them turned over, and then farther up to the shelves of books across the room, the thousand spines, many of them novels. All the lives held there, in every conceivable era, in every state of becoming: of being birthed, of dying, of loving. Of being loved. Well, we are all suckers for a great story; we are practically helpless before them, aren't we, Frith? Frith at eight? Frith at twenty? Frith at thirty-four, with her advanced degrees and her own books?

"Have you read Mutis?" I say. "The Colombian?"

Why on earth did I say that? Was I being cruel? Cruel Queen Frith? I don't think so. I'm really curious.

My eyes go to the drifted snow. I think of James Joyce for the very first time tonight. What took me so long? "The Dead" is one of the saddest stories ever, the couple facing the abyss between them as the snow falls at night over Dublin, over all of Ireland, over all the world, and every attempt at love and true connection. The numbing, the cold, the defeat in the end, always, of heat and life and love. Why I guess I never took to Joyce, for all his mastery. I always felt that beneath the unmatched craft lay the impossibility of enduring love.

Mutis is maybe his antidote. Poor Maqroll, the rogue antihero, haplessly addicted to adventure like Quixote—he succeeded at loving everything far too deeply. My take, for what it's worth.

"No," Willum says. "He's on my list."

My list. I shiver. "Hey," I say gently, "you are possibly the loveliest man still awake in Massachusetts. In New England. Can we talk about all this in the next few days? Give me a minute to digest?"

He laughs—sadly, I think. "Sure," he says. "I guess it's a lot."

"It's a lot," I say.

"Okay, goodnight. Don't let the quack-quacks bite . . ."

Oh, man, did he really just say that? That was a young-dad thing to say. Hayley used to say it. Fuck. "Goodnight, Willum," I say and hang up. More relieved maybe than I should be to end the conversation.

*

We got, finally, to the top of Putney Mountain. It took much longer than it had in the past. The sun was a third of the way up into a clear sky, the air still cool and stirring with a breeze that rose from the other side of the ridge, from the valley of the West River below us, which we could see snaking through its wooded canyon. Beyond it to the west were some of the higher peaks of the Green Mountains, scarred with ski slopes.

We stood on granite bedrock, which shelved out of the moss and wild strawberry that tried to cover it. I loved how the rock made uneven steps and benches. We sat on one, looking east, over the crease of the Connecticut River toward New Hampshire and Mount Monadnock. Nothing but long, successive ridges, wooded hills patched with orchards and fields. The glint of a roof, the red of a barn. And the one lone, proud mountain with its long, patient shoulders and stony top.

I did not know then how the rhythms of this country were imprinting themselves on my being. How the touch, like the lightest fingers, of that cool wind against the back of my ear, my temple, carrying those smells—of the river below, of the leaf-heavy woods, of ripening apples, of sun on granite bedrock and drying moss and the spored scent of warming ferns—how it would tune my senses for the rest of my life. Every wind after that, and every smell carried on the wind, would be compared with the ones that flowed over the two of us in those days.

“Want an orange?” Hayley said. She breathed hard, sucked air deeply on each breath.

“Sure.”

"They're little." She twisted her fanny pack to her tummy and unzipped it, pulled them out. We sat on the ledge, a perfect seat, and we each held a clementine in ten fingers like it was a baby planet, and then we pushed our thumbs into the south pole and broke the skin and began to peel. We never carried water with us. It was heavy, for one, and Hayley subscribed to the Apache custom of tanking up at the watering hole and going all day. For us that meant drinking a quart of water before we took to the woods and sharing long glasses of lemonade when we got back. Hayley made fun of people who carried a liter of filtered water around with them wherever they went.

"What do you think would happen to them if they misplaced it?" she said.

"Dust!" I said. "They'd turn to dust!"

"Correcto." She said that the problem with filtered water is that it has no grit. "How is a pearl made?" she said.

"Grit!" I called.

"How does our immune system get stronger?"

"Grit!"

"Pup, everything worth a crap in this world," she concluded, "is cuz of grit. Almost everything."

"Correcto."

But we often brought fruit, and the little oranges were full of sweet water. Hayley held out her hand for the rind and tucked it back into her belt pack. She reached an arm around my shoulders and pulled me into her and leaned her head on mine. I could feel her heart drumming her rib cage and the deep drafts of her breaths, which were a little frayed at the edges. I could feel the heat of her on the side of my face. She smelled of peppermint soap and her own rich fragrance, which was woodsmoke and something I always thought smelled clean, like sun on haygrass. Her ear snugged over the top of my head.

I closed my eyes. Whatever fears stirred in me were too immense to acknowledge and so I just let myself drift within her encircling arm. We were one being, just one. I felt the wind on my face, the sun, felt the enveloping goodness of my mother, and the uncertainty, barely there, in the way she held me and leaned against me. Why couldn't we be like this, the two of us, the way we were meant to be, until the end of time?

"Hey, hey," she said softly. "Pup, there's a pair of roughlegs. Wow. Look." She shifted and I sat up.

She was pointing east and north, and I saw them in the transparent blue, two shadows: broad-winged hawks gyring in opposite but overlapping circles. One was higher than the other, and they circled and climbed on the currents of heated air, and then the higher hawk stooped. Folded her wings and tucked and dove, straight at a point of intersection with the other—even from here the geometry was breathtaking—and a split second before impacting, her wings spread and she veered away and shot upward. And in the same instant the other tipped over, wing tip pointing at the treetops, and folded too, and dropped, and caught himself on suddenly spread wings. He swooped upward after her and beat the great wings in fast pursuit. Helped by the updraft, he passed her and went higher and wheeled and dove, and then it looked like they were grappling. Both plummeted together, maybe entangled, but they tore themselves apart well above the woods, and then one was fleeing and one in chase, all of it unfolding as they drifted north, probably pushed by the wind.

Was it life and death or play? I couldn't tell. It looked to me like they were having fun.

"Are they playing?" I said.

"I think so."

"Or maybe fighting?"

"Or maybe that's a date," she said.

"Whoa."

"I know. Love is funny."

"That's a fact," I said.

Hayley laughed and pinched my ear. "You wanna fall asleep up here or take the Circle Trail back down and see the goofy sculptures?"

"Let's go see the goofy sculptures."

"Okay," she said. "We can live dangerously and drink from the brook."

"Definitely."

We called it the Circle Trail. It dropped off the back side of the ledgy top of the mountain, toward the West River. We loved that tight little valley. It was much more of a canyon than the Connecticut, and if you dropped all the way down you could cross a red-painted covered bridge to get to the Brookline Road on the other side. But the trail fell only a few hundred feet and then circled back north and east and crossed Sawyer Brook. We often drank, against the stern warnings of everyone, even Rosie, about the dangers of giardia. We were probably both carriers by now anyway, and we never got sick. After the narrow trail crossed the brook, it contoured back to join the one we'd come up, and all along this section were whimsical piles of balanced rocks—not just simple cairns, but little pyramids and henge-like encirclements and elf dominions laid out like the ruins of Mayan cities—flat plaza, courtyard, temple—and also wood benches propped on stones, presumably for resting and contemplating the ephemeral nature of all human endeavor. The whole trail for that half-mile section seemed to carry a rhythm of irony. It was fun, but there was something smart about it that bothered me, bothers me still. As if the woods and the brook themselves weren't enough somehow.

We stood in the sun and wind and allowed the distances to soak into us for another minute, and then we turned and dropped off the back side of the mountain.

*

The next poem, unsurprisingly, is called "Hawks." Hayley would have dug through the five hundred or so of Li Xue's poems to find one that mirrored our time together. That her selection sometimes charted so closely my own memories—should it surprise me? It does. I know we were close, that our hearts, sometimes, as on the mountain, seemed to beat as one. But that she so often chose poems that spoke to my own most treasured recollections—it was as if she herself were speaking from that time and saying, "Pup, hey, do you remember that morning in early September when we saw the roughlegs flying?"

Yes, Hayley, I remember. All on my own.

Hawks

This morning we walked in white fog through the rhododendron
and bamboo,
up and up the narrow trail. The thunder of the first cascade
shook the forest and threw cold spray
and we climbed above it until we could barely hear its music
below.
We stopped when we heard the temple bell toll across the valley.
Our favorite ledge. The mist faded in sunlight. You pointed.
"Look, hawks!" you said.
There were two, wings outstretched, sliding westward, circling
each other and climbing.
They made no effort, grew smaller and smaller until we lost
them
against the western mountains.

Sixteen

There is forgetting, and then there is the deliberate decision not to remember. The next nine days before Hayley's surgery were an exercise in willpower. I willed myself to stay curled in her arms in those cold dawns, to feel her heat, her rough hand haphazard on the side of my face, tucked under an armpit. Willed myself not to move, because I knew even then that this time together, spooned in our bed, would not last. In the loft in the cabin that smelled like woodsmoke and kerosene and bread and Hayley. I willed myself to hold her hand and walk with her down to the pond to check on Mr. Beaver, to walk farther into the woods to see if he had made any improvements to his dam, to see if he had found a mate yet, though neither of us was sure where she would come from or how she would find him.

"Do they call or anything?" I asked her. "They don't howl like a wolf or anything?"

“No, Pup, I don’t think so. I don’t even think they yip like a coyote.”

“Or chirp like a cricket.”

“Right.”

“Or warble.”

“I don’t even think they warble. They do slap their tails, though.”

“Yep.”

“Maybe the sound travels down valley.” She squeezed my hand.

We walked slowly back up to the pond, where we watched the trout making rings like rain on the smooth, dark water.

“Should we fish?” I said. “I could throw the fly I made from Bernie’s feathers.” He was our obnoxious rooster.

“It’d be too easy this morning, wouldn’t it?”

“I guess.”

“Unless you want trout for breakfast.”

I shrugged. Oatmeal with maple syrup and cream from Frazier’s cows seemed just as good.

"Just a sec." She let go of my hand to turn and brace herself and cover her mouth with a forearm. The coughs, the sound of them, the sight of her convulsed, stung me like buckshot. I could not get out of range.

So I willed myself not to fear that she would never come back the same. The surgery would fix whatever was going on, take away the spots on her lungs. But we know things as children we ought not to know, things no one would ever presume to teach us. And so beneath the willfulness and sweetness of those days was a blind fear, and beneath the fear was a darkness without depth, without firelight or starlight or lamplight. And so I held Hayley's hand more tightly and we walked back up the hill and made oatmeal and coffee (Hayley) and hot chocolate (me), and we sat on our bench and watched the lifting sun make long shadows of the apple trees whose fruit was already ripening and felt the first warmth on our faces. And I willed myself to believe that Hayley and I would pick them together, and that Bill would tell us again that they were noncompliant and probably buy them anyway.

Rosie came over some afternoons for horseshoe competitions. Sometimes I was very happy to see her and called to her from the moment I saw whatever bright color was moving through the trees, and sometimes I resented her presence. Sometimes I felt that she was robbing me of an hour with Hayley I would never admit could be stolen. Rosie was incredibly sensitive, and she could sense the shift, and on many days she would stop by to check in and leave it at that. That respect, and her awareness of what this time might mean, were a form of generosity that I would recall later with the deepest love.

So on many of those afternoons it was just the two of us. And Bear. One day we loaded up the truck and drove three hours, all the way to Portland, Maine, so Hayley could show me the ocean. I'd never been to the seashore, not that I could remember. I guess I had been to the Gulf Coast once, when I was two, visiting Pop's family. It was a sunny Tuesday morning in early September, and we stopped for lobster rolls at a shack on a dock, and I remember asking Hayley about the hundreds of colored buoys in the water, and I remember her hair blowing across her face and her wiping the strands to the side and getting butter from the roll all over her nose. She laughed brightly without coughing and she said, "Those are how we got these," and held up the roll.

And then she explained to me the whole system and pointed out the moored lobster boats and said that by two they were mostly done pulling their traps. Crescent Beach was nearly empty. The curve of it, the small surf hitting the sand, the dunes blowing in the sun, the thickets of wild roses. I was enchanted. We spread a blanket and Hayley nodded and I ran headlong into the waves and was tumbled for the first time—a wave broke on me and rolled me onto the shallow hardpack and filled my only bathing suit with sand. I was in thrall. I ran back out and battled the waves again and again, and Bear barked and barked and splashed around in the froth, and I thought it was the best thing ever. Hayley stood finally and stripped to her suit and waded out and showed me how to launch myself to bodysurf.

"It's all timing," she said. "Look, Pup. Get ready. Ready? Now!" And spring. Hands together and arms extended and the first one I actually caught—felt myself lift on the wave and then drop, accelerate, felt it break behind and over me and felt the rush of the glide, right up on the flat until my belly was scraping sand. I came up yelling and Bear was barking and Hayley was shouting, "Wow! Wow! That was truly awesome! You are a surfer like your mom!"

Euphoria. She was standing knee deep in wave wash, arms crossed over her chest and shivering. She was making herself be strong. For me. Grit.

That's the image I see when I close my eyes: Hayley yelling, cheering me on, her arms crossed, holding herself. Behind her, the blowing dunes. Too cold to be there, but there, her body already too thin, shivering.

*

The next part I cannot bear.

The hospital was the dividing line I had felt coming like certain rain. The surgery. The finding of an aggressive cancer, *we think we got all of it . . .* A lump under the arm. Metastasis. Head scarf. My mother growing smaller. Her eyes enlarged in the thinning face, big and shiny and hungry, as if they might absorb everything for the coming journey.

Her return home as the first frosts came at night, whitening the grass like moonlight. The bed downstairs. "I'm sorry I can't sleep with you, Pup. Spoon you like we do."

"That's okay, Mom." Not okay. After two nights alone, I crawled in with her in the narrow bed and her arms came around me and we made do.

We made do, as we always did. And I finally slept through the night.

Coffee made her sick now, so we drank tea together on the porch, on our bench, and watched the apples ripen and drop and watched the maples turn all the gaudy pinks and pulsing oranges, and watched the nor'easter blow in on a cold gray afternoon and slant the rain into the trees and blow the leaves down all over the grass and the road. Mom wrapped in a thick blanket Rosie had woven her, a night blue, Mom's favorite color. Her feet stuffed in double wool socks, also knit by our friend.

And impossibly, sometimes at night, she lit the lantern and sat at her table, though I know the hard chair hurt her, and she addressed herself, all of the self she had, to Li Xue's poems.

I am crying now, in this half-lit crepuscular office, the one standing lamp with its dim bulb looking over my shoulder as if it, too, were curious to see the next poem. Curious? I am not curious. I am as incapable of not turning the next page as I would be of not sleeping. Or grieving. Or wanting.

On Hearing the Cranes Flying South in the Dark

My daughter is old enough now to find her way through
the thickets of the Three Teachings and the poems of the masters.

When we hear a flute through the trees at end of day
she can turn from the gate and say
"Wild Geese Descending on Level Sand," or "Evening Temple
Bell,"
or "Plum Blossoms." She knows that the Way, like water,
prefers the low places. She moves the way a deer moves
at water's edge when she thinks no one is watching.
I am watching of course! I see her in mist, in rain.
I hear her sing as she gathers in the garden.
Autumn comes swiftly.
Before the frost whitens the grass I want to hear her sing
"High Mountains and Flowing Water."

*

What she wanted: to hear her daughter sing.

We tend, when someone close to us is dying, to focus on our own desires. Not only as children do we do this, but as adults too. It is terribly selfish. The desire that this person not go away, not ever. That she stay close, that she hold us, that she be there to listen when we have something to report, or when we are heartbroken. That she smooth our hair, or rumple it, or pull at the knots. That she laugh at our insights. That she is there, always. How rarely do we dare to imagine what she might want: another morning with fog thick in the valley like cotton. Another pestering question from her young daughter. Another cup of tea. A night to spoon. A poem.

Seventeen

Fair to say, I didn't know what to do with these emotions. Sci-Fi brought venison and Ben up one morning and he sat on the bench with Hayley and he told her about the war the Raiders had had with the Quebecois Hells Angels. She told me about it later. I could hear her laughing and coughing from where Ben and I were trying to pick apples with the picking ladder.

None of the Raiders could cross the border into Canada, because they all had warrants and they'd be ID'd and run through the computer at the gate and arrested. At first the two gangs had worked together, swapping drugs and money through couriers—drugs going north mostly and money south—but there'd been a falling-out over payments and then a war. They couldn't cross to get at each other, so they went to Emmetville, a village on the Maine border that straddles both sides. There's a stone curb that runs through town and marks the boundary. He said it was like third grade, with both gangs standing on either side of the line and hurling insults and getting up in each other's beards, and within minutes the state troopers on one side and the Mounties on the other were swarming the place like bees to honey. Sci-Fi said the cops stayed out of it, making a kind of a Boys Will Be Boys perimeter with their SUVs and squad cars, until an Angel pulled out a .357 and shot Sci-Fi's good friend Leo in the hip. He said the mayhem that ensued was compounded by the fact that the troopers were absolutely forbidden from taking enforcement action in Canada and vice versa, a legal fine point that the Mounties strictly adhered to and the troopers ignored. Which caused international screaming matches and scuffles among the cops, Grays against the Reds. Sci-Fi claimed that bikers are a lot smarter than they used to be, and nowadays nobody, "*No*-bo-dy," wants to stack time, and so in the mass confusion, most of the gang members on both sides ran to their bikes, hopped on, and roared away. Leo, who'd been shot, recovered enough to ride, and only four bikers out of forty got arrested, and all were let off due to jurisdictional conflicts and gross infractions of national and international due process. And the two gangs patched up their differences and used the incident to smooth out their distribution procedures.

"So: All's well that ends well!" Hayley was laughing when she told me the story, and holding her ribs. "Not what he said," she sputtered. "He said, 'So, go fucking figure. Turned out *alll*-right in the fucking end.' "

Meanwhile, I'd ordered Ben to hold the shaky ladder while I climbed with the sack and he got distracted by a red newt and forgot and I almost fell off. I hustled down the ladder and screamed at him and shoved him to the tall grass and kicked his leg. He didn't cry or resist, he just stared up at me wide-eyed like I was some species of animal he'd never seen before. I was the only one in school that had never been mean to him, never betrayed him. I think about it to this day. That look. At 3:30 a.m. when I can't sleep, that's one of the images that haunt me.

*

Rosie came over most afternoons. There was nothing spoken. I think, because she was super sensitive, that she wanted to leave the mornings to the two of us. The first cups of tea, the quiet sitting on the bench wrapped in blankets. Hayley wasn't hungry for breakfast and I was happy with a bowl of rolled oats and dried apples, with honey and boiling water poured on top and a splash of fresh cream. I didn't understand the demands of chemo, neither the schedule nor the rationale, but three days a week in that first month Rosie drove Hayley to the hospital in Brattleboro for her torture sessions. It left her nauseous and her hair came out in the brush. By the time the brilliant leaves were spilling out of the trees, Hayley called it off. Enough. She had had a good private talk with Dr. Dixon and they'd come to an agreement. So she could stay home, and I think it was some comfort to her that her weakness now was from the disease, not the treatment.

She slept more. Rosie came over and she stayed with her for hours, reading novels out loud, and she played horseshoes with me. On fine afternoons, Hayley roused and came out on the porch and I saw her reaching for the edge of the counter, for the doorframe, trying to move as smoothly as she could to hide her increasing frailty. She would sit on the porch on the bench and referee. One turn in one game, Rosie threw two ringers and all my throws went wild. On my last throw the shoe turned sideways in the air and cartwheeled off the little shelf of our pit and down the hill into the brown grass of the orchard and Hayley exclaimed a loud "Haaaaw!"—she threw her energy into her voice whenever she could—and I just watched the errant shoe disappear in the grass, and Hayley called, "Frith, hon, you need to recalibrate!" I stood in my old dress and burst into tears.

Rosie had me in her arms before I could work up any snot, and Hayley was stricken speechless and I cried harder, noticing her silence.

Recalibrate is exactly what I needed to do and didn't know how. That night, after Rosie walked down to her car in the dark and drove away, we went to bed early and I slept hard and dreamless, but awoke sometime in the middle of the night and found Hayley's arms around me as always, but they were shaking just a little, and then I could hear her crying. Trying so hard to be silent, her face in the back of my nightie where I could feel the dampness, and I lay as still as I could.

The leaves fell and in early November we had a light night snowfall. Three days before Thanksgiving I woke up in the dark and felt Hayley's arms around me and I slipped from them to pee. I almost stepped on Bear, who was whining. When I got back into bed, she did not shift to welcome me. I moved her right arm gently to worm beneath it and it was heavy and I crawled in close and I whispered, "Hayley, in the morning let's wrap ourselves in our blankets and drink our tea on the porch." I pushed my back against her and I held her right arm around me with both of mine. At first light I slipped out again and I poured the kettle full of water and lit the gas burner and I made tea for both of us.

I wouldn't look at the bed. It was cold in the cabin. I knocked open the door to the woodstove and kicked up the coals with the short poker and added smaller chunks of split wood and left the door cracked the way Hayley had taught me, until I could hear the fluttering rush of the draft and the flames catching. I let the tea bags steep and added honey and cream the way we liked it and carried the mugs to the table and put hers in front of her chair. Wisps of steam came off it as it did every morning. There was frost on the lower windowpanes and it was grainy and stained rose with sunrise. I blew on my tea so I wouldn't burn my tongue and then I remembered to let Bear out—he wouldn't stop whimpering and kept bumping my knees—and then I brought out two blankets and both mugs and I sat on the bench in the icy dawn and drank the tea and watched my breath smoke. When the sun rose enough to melt the frost in the grass I called Bear and we walked down the hill to Ivy's and used her phone to call Rosie.

Eighteen

We had a service in the orchard in the first week of December. Bill from the co-op came, and Sci-Fi and Ben, and Ivy Darrow and Florence Watts and her husband, Wit, and Frazier Copper-Ellis, and the Osgoods, Doc Dixon, Marie, Hy Kyung Brandt and her husband, Vinn, and their three kids, who were all in high school, and a dozen others we'd gotten to know from delivering Cajun lunches. And three academics from Boston, two women and a man, who had also been in Jackson Hole at the conference, and an old translator of Li Bai and Du Fu whom Hayley had talked about often. His name was Creek, and he was ancient and stooped and walked with an aluminum hiking pole with a spike at the end. Which was good, because though there was less than a foot of snow on the ground, the days had thawed and then frozen, and it was very icy. Chris Osgood had plowed a clearing in the trees down to grass and a walking path, and he'd sanded it heavily so no one would fall.

Rosie spoke. I couldn't hear anything she said for the rushing in my ears, which was like a flooded brook. But then she pulled out a sheet of lined paper and unfolded it and said, "Some of you know Hayley was working on another book by the poetess Li Xue, who lived in China in the eighth century. This is one I think she translated in the last couple of weeks. It's called 'Winter Brook.' "

Winter Brook

When I climb above the brook flying from purple cliffs,
through the wind in pines, the lonely bell,
and cross the creek, and climb
into the streaming mists, and past them,
and hear the geese descending in clouds—
when I find myself humming "Sail Returning from Distant
Shore"
and feel the cold breath of the snows in the pass,
then I will stop before going over and turn
and I will raise this empty wooden cup to you, my dearest
companion:

How many cups of spring water have we shared? How many
cups of wine?

Tonight I will be so far away. We will not light the candles
together.
Tomorrow only the sky and the mountains will be between us.

I listened as if Hayley were whispering it right into my ear. I know now that Li Xue might have been addressing another poet, a friend, a lover, the earth, even life, even the Way. But on that bright winter day I could almost feel Mom's breath brushing my temple, and I knew that the poem was chosen for me.

Epilogue

The clouds are running this morning. South to north in fast fleets that grow denser and darker. It smells like rain, and I have no doubt the rain will come and tear the blossoms out of the apple trees in tender blizzards. I shift my butt on the bench so that I can lean back. It's not that I am huge, but I am learning to accommodate the not-quite-volleyball-size swell that is Hayley Rose. She is right now a noncompliant volleyball. Or soccer ball. She is a kicker, as I was, according to Hayley, and she is making sleepy attempts right now. I sit on Hayley's side of the bench and palm a cup of hot tea—decaffeinated.

The second weekend in New York was all it took. I knew beforehand but went anyway. Willum seemed more desperate the more noticeably with child I became, and I did not have the strength three weeks ago to break his heart. Was it because I'd felt a little nauseated for days? How did Frith the Nordic Queen, who took no prisoners, become such a wimp when it came to love? I went to the brunch on Seventh Avenue in Park Slope, blocks from his airy apartment—I'm getting that his parents have money—and we held hands on the subway. We got out near Brooklyn Bridge Park and strolled slowly along the river walk, from the carousel under the bridge to the rough-plank dock where I think Whitman embarked on "Crossing Brooklyn Ferry." We walked down to the first pier with the basketball courts and skating rink and *didn't* rent Rollerblades—what if I fell?

And the whole time, my slight nausea was maybe knowing that this would not, no way, ever work out. Despite his sweetness. Despite the hipness of his hood, the incontestable glamour and grit of the city, the culture, the food, the every-language-spoken-on-every-corner, the undeniable and continuing evidence that this boy was a man capable of caring and responsibility, the inescapable smell of old money and what that might mean for my child—our child.

Sometimes we know. We usually do, loud and clear. I knew. Even after my talk with Donny Spellman, who said he was sure he could get me through the committee at Columbia. A truly great department. I lay in Willum's bed under his skylight with the sound, yes, of a cricket in the garden and let him stroke me gently and not demand a thing, and I felt the terrifying jaws of the steel spring trap that Hayley would never let Sci-Fi set for Mr. Beaver. The underwater chain, the inability to breathe. I felt panic.

In Penn Station, he bought me flowers. On the dirty platform with a current of passengers rushing by to their train cars, he blushed into his shirt in the way that charms me and fluttered his eyelashes and forced a smile and said, "This is going to work. We are going to have the happiest family, who would've thought?"

Who would've thought. I knew. That evening I drove down to a boat launch on the Connecticut north of Amherst, a dirt-and-gravel ramp in the trees at the edge of a cornfield, a place that reminds me of the river at Putney and settles me; and with the current slipping by—dark water floating with twigs and leaves—I called him and told him I was sticking to plan A. "I care for you," I said. "But I know that I have to raise my daughter *here*, by myself. And I know that you have a rich life in New York ahead of you."

The "here" I meant was not Amherst, but Here. Here where I am now, in the cabin in the orchard where my mother raised me. This is my home.

*

The rain will fall by noon. I have been here long enough to know the weather like a farmer. I know the smell, the freshness of the wind, the sound of it in the hardwoods behind the cabin, and the way it soughs in the tall old pine at the corner. It will rain. Good. And the temperature will drop, and if the clouds clear tonight, which I'm guessing they will, the sky will teem with stars and a stillness will settle in the newly leafed forest and it will come close to frost but won't. A reprieve for the blossoms that are thick in the trees, and the fruit. And I'll light a fire in the old woodstove and make a late herbal tea and sit out here wrapped in one of Rosie's old blankets, the night-blue one, and I'll linger long after the tea is gone. I'll feel you kick and sleep and shift and be as entertained by your willfulness as by the sound of the brook.

Rosie took me. When Mom died, she took me in without hesitation, without even a discussion, both of us understanding the rightness of it. I moved in with her and Marie in the big yellow house with the blue door. And Bear. He loved Marie, and since he shouldered and bumped the ones he loved, he had to be trained not to knock her over. She taught me the piano. Her dementia came on in short bouts and passed. The second day after I moved in, I came down from my hastily prepared room. I had only one small duffel of clothes; the framed picture of me and Hayley, wet and grinning wide, heads together, at the quarry, and the one of Pop, standing in his johnboat, smiling shyly in the dappled light of the swamp; the green blanket Rosie had woven for me. Marie was sitting on the piano bench with a benign smile. She said, "Wanna try?" She was as white as the ivory keys. She placed my fingers. Her sunspotted hands trembled and were as light as small birds, but surprisingly strong. She moved my fingers in time through a scale and I was gone. Taken.

That's how I bonded with Marie, and for the next year and a half until she passed, we didn't say much but we played together a lot, on the bench, side by side.

Rosie was Rosie. We decided I would go to school full-time and she drove me the six miles down every morning, and I actually liked it. The consistency of showing up every day, the growing friendships. Ben became more and more isolated, and seemed to prefer it that way, but I kept an eye on him and ate lunch with him once in a while.

A few nights a week, randomly, when the weather was enticing or stormy, Rosie did not continue down the long straightaway on the Westminster West Road, but waved to Sci-Fi and the brothers at the corner and turned up Tavern Hill and drove to the cabin and we spent the night. We lit the stove, we played horseshoes, we fished in the pond, in the brook. Even when it wasn't warm enough, we swam, and we ran naked back into the cabin and stood shivering by the woodstove.

Bear loved these interludes. He loved being at the cabin more than anything, and I learned to look away when he bounded out of the car and whined, and zigzagged, sniffing everything, searching for Hayley, hoping this time she'd be there.

I was happiest there. I am happiest here now. I will keep the house in Northampton for the two days of teaching, but we will live here.

*

Rosie was my best friend after Bear. A good surrogate. When I was fourteen, she enrolled me in the Putney School, which was only a mile from the orchard, and I adored the place, the serious attention to the arts, working in the dairy barn, the outdoor trips. I loved being a day student and being able to have my friends over to Westminster West, and with Rosie's assent I spent some nights at the cabin by myself. My best friend at school was a foreign student from China named Mei Yan. She knew the Tang poets and loved them, and even knew the most famous poems of Li Xue. Maybe that's why I decided she would be my friend. She was very shy, she was a serious flutist, and she had never been camping until her fall trip in the White Mountains. Once in a while I dared to accompany her on the piano, and she teased me gently. Sophomore year, we got permission from the dorm head and I invited her to the cabin for a night and she fell head over heels. She couldn't get over that we were lighting a kerosene lantern, a woodstove. Mei is still my best friend. She plays with the Amsterdam Symphony Orchestra, and she married a serious Dutch biologist, but I talk to her almost every month and visit when I can. Last year she brought her own young daughter, Kim, to the orchard for a week.

When I got my driver's license, and with an unspoken understanding from Rosie, I began to spend more time at the cabin, maybe half my nights. The school didn't know about it—I'm not sure they would have approved, I was only sixteen—but I loved it, I needed it. I slept up in the loft in our old bed, and I curled on my left side as I always used to do, and I imagined Hayley's arm thrown around me and I felt comforted.

I studied Spanish and literature and then Spanish literature, then the works of Latin America, and I went as far as the good teachers at Putney could take me. One Saturday night in June, Rosie and I were eating outside on the patio of the yellow house. We were swatting away blackflies; I could see them trying to burrow into Rosie's thick blond hair, and Bear was snapping at them and generally irritated, and I asked her if it was okay to love the Colombian, Álvaro Mutis, so much and not, say, Mo Yan. Rosie put down her fork and unconsciously adjusted her rimless hexagonal glasses. She pursed her lips.

"You're thinking of Hayley?"

I nodded.

"Hayley wants you to be your own person. That's all she wants." She blinked and took off the glasses and polished them with the tail of her flannel shirt. She settled them back on and smiled at me through whatever emotion and said, "The only way to do that is to follow your nose. Follow what you love, always. It's the best way to stay safe."

I've thought about that often. It's what Hayley gave to me, and what Li Xue gave to her: That we are of this earth. All of us. That if we stay close to her, and to what we truly love, we will be okay.

*

I got into grad school in California. I loved the coast, San Francisco, Marin, and especially the wild cliffs and beaches of Big Sur, and all the literary history there. I drove down whenever I could and hiked the hills and swam in the turbulent pocket coves. In late November of my third year, I got a call from Ivy Darrow. She said, "Frith, Rosie's had an accident."

"An accident? When?"

"Tonight. She was driving to the cabin, up Tavern Hill . . ."

"Yes?"

"Well, it was dark—it is dark—and the first snow of the year had put down a couple of inches and slicked the road . . ."

"Ivy, what?"

"I'm sorry." I heard the huff. "She was at Brelsford Corner and a bunch of the bikers from below—that bunch that you and Hayley befriended—they were coming down from a party up on the mountain and two skidded out and lost control. They drifted into her and she swerved away and went over the bank."

"What?" I stammered. "Where is she?"

"Well." Static. "She died."

She died. I stood outside the Nepalese restaurant on Lytton in Palo Alto and gasped for air. That was one thing that was never going to happen, that was definitely not supposed to happen. I passed out, right there on the sidewalk, and was revived by three strangers and two Nepali waiters.

She died. Grimm and a Raider named Tuner lived, thank God.

I caught a red-eye to Hartford that night, rented a car and drove up. I never saw her. She was broken badly in the wreck and Ivy ID'd her for the coroner and we held a service at the Grange in Brattleboro, where she'd often shown and sold her hangings. She'd grown up in Saxtons River and was a fixture in the area and there may have been two hundred people. I slept in the cabin that night. I turned onto my left side and I felt the emptiness behind me as I had so many times, and I whispered for a long time to Hayley and Rosie. *Wherever you guys are, I know you're together.* Bear had gone my first year at Stanford, but I kept waking up, thinking I was hearing him whimper, his claws on the wood of the floor. It was the wind in the stovepipe.

I sold Rosie's place. More and more well-to-do back-to-the-landers were moving into the area—who could blame them?—and it sold for a lot. I finished my PhD. I got a professorship at Amherst.

I am pregnant.

I am here now. On the bench, our bench. If I turn away, I can almost imagine Hayley next to me. *Pup, rouse yourself. Go get some exercise. I never had to say that to you before. Little Feisty in your belly will appreciate it too.*

I can hear the brook. I know by the rush it is running high. I know what the little ledge drop will look like just by the sound. I know that the water will be sieving through Mr. Beaver's dam, now maintained by what I'm guessing are his great-grandchildren. They lumber over and into the pond once in a while and I beg them not to screw with it in any way and they aren't afraid of me in the least. *You should be,* I murmur. *I am Frith, queen of this place.*

Acknowledgments

I am deeply grateful to my first readers, without whom this book would not have been written. Kim Yan, Helen Thorpe, Donna Gershten, and Lisa Jones shared, as always, their insight, energy, and enthusiasm. As did Geordie Heller, beloved cousin.

Thanks to Suzanne Heller and Jim Lefevre for guidance on birds, and to doctors Mitchell Gershten and Melissa Gillespie for advice on all things medical. I am grateful to Haifeng Ye, Gabby Masucci, Isaac Savitz, Li Peters, and Catherine Shoeffler for their input, and ever thankful to the spectacular translator Céline Leroy for helping me to understand the process of translation.

I raise a glass to my original editors at Scribd, Mark Bryant and Laura Hohnhold, who were with me when I was a kid and are with me again. Such an honor. And thanks so much to Jenny Jackson for giving the novel renewed life.

It has been one of the great privileges and pleasures of my life to work with David Halpern, who shepherded the novel from the beginning as early reader and then as agent.

And lastly, I wish to thank Kenneth Rexroth, W. S. Merwin, and Red Pine for their exquisite work in translating from the Chinese some of the most beautiful poetry ever written.

ALSO BY

PETER HELLER

THE GUIDE

Kingfisher Lodge, nestled in a canyon on a mile and a half of the most pristine river water on the planet, is known by locals as "Billionaire's Mile" and is locked behind a heavy gate. Sandwiched between barbed wire and a meadow with a sign that reads "Don't Get Shot!" the resort boasts boutique fishing at its finest. Safe from viruses that have plagued America for years, Kingfisher offers a respite for wealthy clients. Now it also promises a second chance for Jack, a return to normalcy after a young life filled with loss. When he is assigned to guide a well-known singer, his only job is to rig her line, carry her gear, and steer her to the best trout he can find. But then a human scream pierces the night, and Jack soon realizes that this idyllic fishing lodge may merely be a cover for a far more sinister operation. A novel as gripping as it is lyrical, as frightening as it is moving, *The Guide* is another masterpiece from Peter Heller.

Fiction

THE PAINTER

After having shot a man in a Santa Fe bar, the famous artist Jim Stegner served his time and has since struggled to manage the dark impulses that sometimes overtake him. Now he lives a quiet life—until the day that he comes across a hunting guide beating a small horse, and a brutal act of new violence rips his quiet life right open. Pursued by men dead set on retribution, Jim is left with no choice but to return to New Mexico and the high-profile life he left behind, where he'll reckon with past deeds and the dark shadows in his own heart.

Fiction

CELINE

Celine is not your typical private eye. With prep school pedigree and a pair of opera glasses for stakeouts, her methods are unconventional but extremely successful. Working out of her jewel box of an apartment nestled under the Brooklyn Bridge, Celine has made a career out of tracking down missing persons nobody else can find. But when a young woman named Gabriela employs her expertise, what was meant to be Celine's last case becomes a scavenger hunt through her own memories, the secrets there, and the surprising redemptions. Gabriela's father was a *National Geographic* photographer who went missing in Wyoming twenty years ago, and while he was assumed to have been mauled by a grizzly, his body was never found. Celine and her partner set out to Yellowstone National Park to follow a trail gone cold but soon realize that somebody desperately wants to keep this case closed. Combining ingenious plotting with crystalline prose and sweeping natural panoramas, Peter Heller gives us his finest work to date.

Fiction

ALSO AVAILABLE

Burn
The Dog Stars
Hell or High Water (eBook Only)
The Last Ranger
The Orchard
The River